DATE DUE		

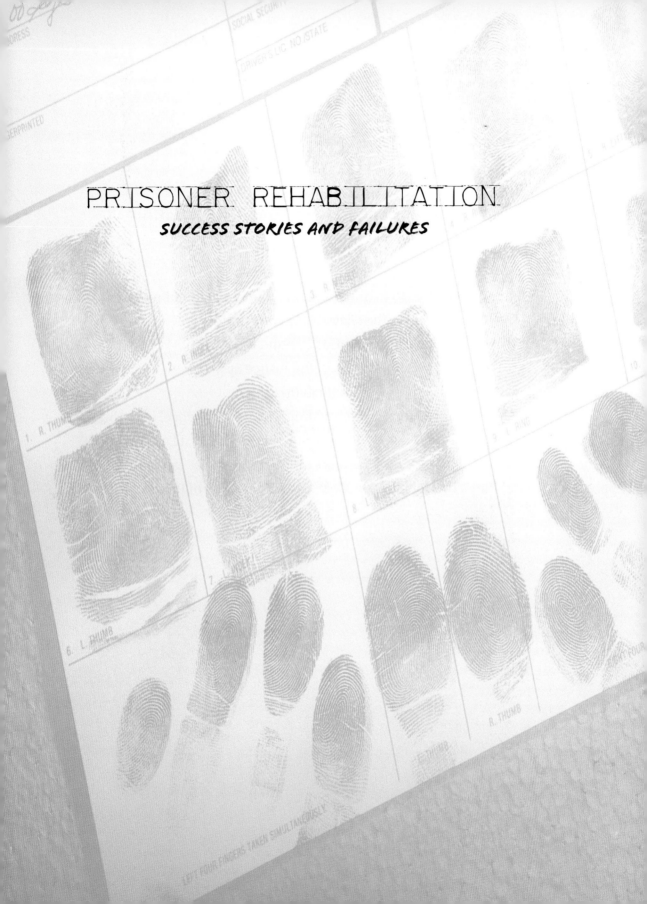

PRISONER REHABILITATION
SUCCESS STORIES AND FAILURES

Incarceration Issues:
Punishment, Reform, and Rehabilitation

TITLE LIST

PRISONER REHABILITATION
SUCCESS STORIES AND FAILURES

by Joan Esherick

Mason Crest Publishers
Philadelphia

Mason Crest Publishers Inc.
370 Reed Road
Broomall, Pennsylvania 19008
(866) MCP-BOOK (toll free)

#89232

13 12 11 10 09 08   10 9 8 7 6 5 4 3 2

Mason Crest 7/10   9/3/10 *22.95

Library of Congress Cataloging-in-Publication Data

Esherick, Joan.
  Prisoner rehabilitation : success stories and failures / by Joan Esherick.
    p. cm. — (Incarceration issues)
  Includes bibliographical references and index.
  ISBN 1-59084-994-9   ISBN 1-59084-984-1 (series)
  ISBN 978-1-59084-994-1   ISBN 978-1-59084-984-2 (series)

  1. Criminals—Rehabilitation—United States—Juvenile literature. 2.
Prisons—United States—Juvenile literature. I. Title. II. Series.
  HV9304.E75 2007
  365.66—dc22

                  2006001473

Interior design by MK Bassett-Harvey.
Interiors produced by Harding House Publishing Service, Inc.
www.hardinghousepages.com

Cover design by Peter Spires Culotta.

Printed in Malaysia.

CONTENTS

INTRODUCTION

by Larry E. Sullivan, Ph.D.

Prisons will be with us as long as we have social enemies. We will punish them for acts that we consider criminal, and we will confine them in institutions.

Prisons have a long history, one that fits very nicely in the religious context of sin, evil, guilt, and expiation. In fact, the motto of one of the first prison reform organizations was "Sin no more." Placing offenders in prison was, for most of the history of the prison, a ritual for redemption through incarceration; hence the language of punishment takes on a very theological cast. The word "penitentiary" itself comes from the religious concept of penance. When we discuss prisons, we are dealing not only with the law but with very strong emotions and reactions to acts that range from minor or misdemeanor crimes to major felonies like murder and rape.

Prisons also reflect the level of the civilizing process through which a culture travels, and it tells us much about how we treat our fellow human beings. The great nineteenth-century Russian author Fyodor Dostoyevsky, who was a political prisoner, remarked, "The degree of civilization in a society can be measured by observing its prisoners." Similarly, Winston Churchill, the great British prime minister during World War II, said that the "treatment of crime and criminals is one of the most unfailing tests of civilization of any country."

Since the very beginnings of the American Republic, we have attempted to improve and reform the way we imprison criminals. For much of the history of the American prison, we tried to rehabilitate or modify the criminal behavior of offenders through a variety of treatment programs. In the last quarter of the twentieth century, politicians and citizens alike realized that this attempt had failed, and we began passing stricter laws, imprisoning people for longer terms and building more prisons. This movement has taken a great toll on society. Approximately two million people are behind bars today. This movement has led to the overcrowding of prisons, worse living conditions, fewer educational programs, and severe budgetary problems. There is also a significant social cost, since imprisonment splits families and contributes to a cycle of crime, violence, drug addiction, and poverty.

All these are reasons why this series on incarceration issues is extremely important for understanding the history and culture of the United States. Readers will learn all facets of punishment: its history; the attempts to rehabilitate offenders; the increasing number of women and juveniles in prison; the inequality of sentencing among the races; attempts to find alternatives to incarceration; the high cost, both economically and morally, of imprisonment; and other equally important issues. These books teach us the importance of understanding that the prison system affects more people in the United States than any institution, other than our schools.

8

PRISONS: PLACES OF PUNISHMENT, PROTECTION, AND POSSIBILITIES

*This is my home now. I've grown up here. The people inside are my **surrogate** family. I try to keep my thoughts more on the inside. When I think about the outs—the world beyond the walls—the pressure starts.*

I realize I can't experience the small things in life. I can't go outside. I can't feel the grass beneath my feet. I can't smell a new rain. I can't be brushed by a breeze. I can't touch a tree.

Sometimes it gets so hard, I think about killing myself. I get nervous knowing people on the outside judge me. They think I'm a monster.

But I'm still a person.
I have feelings.
And I am so sorry.

—seventeen-year-old Sean, incarcerated for murdering his mother, as quoted in *Hard Time: A Real Life Look at Juvenile Crime and Violence.*

I can still remember the first time I entered the death-row cell I was told would be mine. I saw a tiny, dingy white room, four by four feet, with steel bars, a sink, a toilet, a bunk, and a concrete floor.

I was surprised the cell was so small. To step through its barred door, I had to turn my bulky body sideways. In fact, I looked bigger than the entire cell. When I tried to do some push-ups on the floor, I couldn't do them. The gap between the wall and bunk is too narrow for my torso. So I have to do my exercise on top of the bunk, which is the widest space in the cell.

There are no tables or chairs to sit on in the cell, so I have to invent what I need. I sleep on a mattress on the floor because the bunk—a flat rectangle of solid steel welded to four short metal legs, each bolted to the floor—is only six feet long, two and one-half feet wide. That's too small for my body. So I sleep on the floor to keep from falling off the bunk at night and hurting myself. I use the top of the bunk as a table to study, write, draw or exercise. When I need a chair, I roll up the mattress and use it for a seat. It's very uncomfortable at times, but it's this or nothing.

In addition to the cramped quarters, I had to get used to the noise. . . . If the noise doesn't bother you in prison, then surely the funk—or smell—will.

—San Quentin inmate and Nobel Peace Prize nominee Stanley "Tookie" Williams, in his book, *Life in Prison.*

Behind me the steel door hissed and rolled—thwunk—a tomb being sealed. I climbed up on the steel bed, which was bolted to the concrete cell wall. Grateful to be unshackled for the first time since my arrest, I stretched out on the steel slab, waiting, wondering if the cop would come back with some kind of mattress or sheets or even a blanket.

PRISONER REHABILITATION

Tookie Williams was executed on December 13, 2005.

Closed my eyes.
And wept like a lost child.

—forty-seven-year-old Jimmy A. Lerner, a husband, father, and former
   corporate strategic planner incarcerated for voluntary manslaughter, on
   entering his first cell—Suicide Watch 3, or SW3—as quoted in his book,
   You Got Nothing Coming: Notes from a Prison Fish

Though the experiences described in these comments may be foreign
to you, they are made by real people who never thought they'd end up
behind bars. Their experiences are more common than you might think.

The U.S. Department of Justice (DOJ) Bureau of Justice Statistics recorded that as of October 2002, more that two million men and women
were living in incarceration facilities in the United States. That's about 715
adults per 100,000 of the U.S. population, or nearly one out of every fourteen adults living in the United States. A year earlier, according to Canada's solicitor general, Canadian prisons housed over 36,024 inmates, or

Prison conditions are often dismal.

about 116 adult prisoners for every 100,000 Canadians. That's equivalent to nearly one out of a thousand. The International Centre for Prison Studies' World Prison Brief ranks the United States and Canada first and second in highest prison population totals in North America. When looking at the entire world and its 210 countries, Canada is number forty-one—and the United States is number one. The Land of the Free imprisons more people within her borders than any other country on Earth.

How can that be? Some experts suggest that many people in North America end up in prison because, since they can't afford lawyers, they plead guilty to the crimes for which they've been charged. Others suggest that high ***incarceration rates*** result from so many repeat offenders (people who have been jailed, are released, then commit crimes again) returning to prison for lack of adequate alternative placements that would help them transition to life in society. Still others insist that repeat offenders want to go back to prison because the security and opportunities they experience behind bars are greater than what they have on the street. While these assumptions may be true in part, none paints the entire picture. The root of high North American incarceration rates is a complex issue that won't be solved in this book, but one thing is for certain, no matter what the cause: people don't plan to go to prison. Children don't want to become prisoners when they grow up, the way they hope to become doctors or models or basketball stars. No one makes prison his life's goal or ambition. It's never a person's first lifestyle choice.

Prison is *not* fun; it isn't glamorous; it isn't cool; it isn't a manly right of passage. It isn't a free ticket to medical care or education as some people think. Most prisoners will tell you that life behind bars is less than they hoped it would be and far worse than they imagined, especially early in their prison experiences while they were still "fresh fish," or "yellow fish," as new prisoners are called.

Though the daily life of a prisoner varies depending on the prisoner's age, physical size, appearance, health, education, gender, criminal record, ***sentence***, and type of incarceration facility, all prisoners share some experiences in common: fear, isolation, loneliness, loss of freedom, boredom, intimidation, anger, the drive to survive, and the need to learn the rules of "doing time."

Life behind prison fences is not easy.

And that's just it: they are all "doing time" for something. To be incarcerated—put in prison or confined to jail—an individual must have been arrested for or have committed a crime. Some prisoners are only detainees who are kept—detained—in **holding cells** while they wait for their trials. (They've been arrested but have not yet gone to court.) Most prisoners are "convicts" or "cons" who have been found guilty—"convicted"—of a crime and sentenced to live in prison or jail for various periods of time. What kind of sentence, where it will be served, in what type of facility, and for how long are determined by sentencing guidelines used by the judge and jury who served in the convict's trial.

Though we commonly use the terms "prison" and "jail" interchangeably, they refer to different incarceration facilities. A *jail* is typically a local facility located in or near the town of a prisoner's arrest. Jails can be

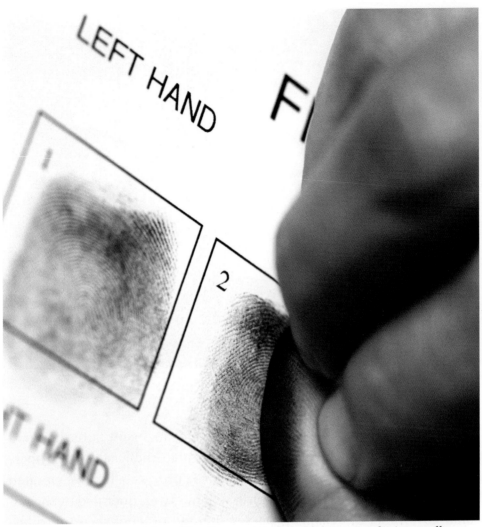

When a person is arrested, he will be fingerprinted—whether or not he is actually guilty of a crime.

run by the county government (a county jail) or a local borough, town, or city government (the town jail or city jail), and usually house people awaiting their trials or nonviolent convicts who have been sentenced to short periods of time (a few months, for example). Jails are not intended to hold prisoners for long terms, nor are they intended to house violent criminals.

A county jail offers short-term housing for prisoners.

North American *prisons*, on the other hand, are institutions designed to hold prisoners for longer stays, and they are usually state run (operated by individual states in the United States), provincially run (operated by individual provinces in Canada), or federally run (operated by the national government). Prisons provide different levels of security (minimum, low, medium, or maximum) and house inmates who best fit their targeted prison population. A violent criminal convicted of committing a brutal crime during which people were hurt or killed would be housed in a prison designed for inmates prone to violence (a maximum-security prison or supermax facility). A criminal convicted of a nonviolent crime, such as check forgery or drug possession, might be sent to a low- or minimum-security prison with other prisoners who are less prone to hurting others.

The difference between security levels is determined by what kind of security devices surround the prison (fences, walls, towers, razor wire,

MANY PLACES OF CONFINEMENT

- **pretrial detention centers:** short-term, local facilities used to hold people until they go to trial or, if found guilty, to hold them until they transfer to the proper facility
- **community correction centers:** same as above, but can be used for longer term, low-security sentences
- **halfway houses:** low-security, supervised-living, community-based homes where convicts can transition from prison to life on the outside
- **house arrest:** confinement at home while wearing an electric monitoring device
- **jails:** local lockups usually affiliated with the local or county police
- **prisons:** state, provincially, or federally run secure (guarded) facilities of various levels of security
- **mental institutions:** residential facilities (some secure) used to house or treat people with mental illness
- **medical referral centers:** places where inmates are sent for medical care
- **boot camps:** short-term, intensive programs (often run outdoors) designed to teach convicts mental and physical discipline

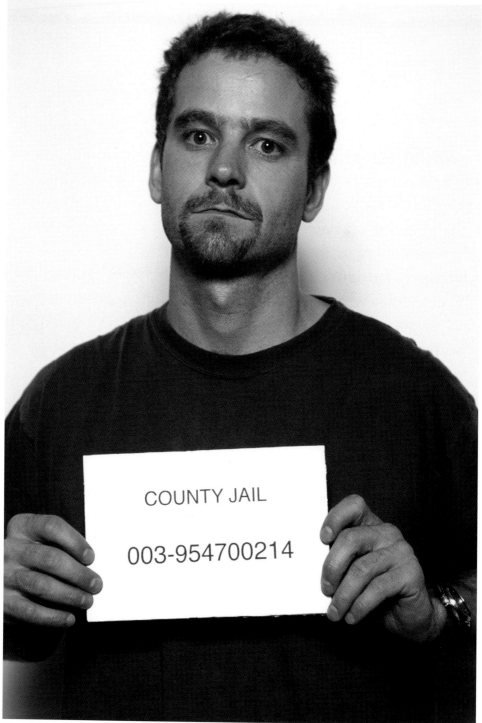

COUNTY JAIL

003-954700214

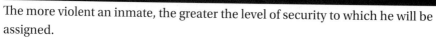

The more violent an inmate, the greater the level of security to which he will be assigned.

A high-security prison will be monitored by multiple security cameras.

armed guards, patrol officers, etc.), how many staff officers work there compared to how many prisoners, what kind of security and monitoring devices protect the inside of the prison (security cameras, barred doors, bulletproof glass, tiers, monitoring stations, etc.), and its type of inmate living quarters (open cells with bars, secure cells with solid walls and doors, dormitories where many inmates live together, single rooms, double rooms, etc.). The more violent an inmate is (or his crime is), the greater the security will be in his assigned facility.

Proneness toward violence isn't the only criteria for determining where a convict will serve his time. Sometimes his likelihood of *rehabilitation* plays a role. According to the Federal Bureau of Prisons (FBOP), the purpose of putting people in prisons and jails isn't just punishment (although this is indeed part of the reasoning behind incarceration); it is

also to help prisoners learn what they need to learn to become contributing members of society. The FBOP Mission Statement says it this way:

> It is the mission of the Federal Bureau of Prisons to protect society by confining offenders in the controlled environments of prisons and community-based facilities that are safe, humane, cost-efficient, and appropriately secure, and that provide work and other self-improvement opportunities to assist offenders in becoming law-abiding citizens.

Prisons and jails, when run well, can be places of positive influence and change—places where inmates can learn to read, learn a trade, graduate from high school, or take college classes. These correctional institutions can offer opportunities for growth and education the convicts might not have on the street or in the neighborhoods from which they come. In order to be rehabilitated—to become a socially healthy, constructive, law-abiding individual—a prisoner may need to learn new ways of thinking, coping, and living, all of which can be taught through proper reeducation programs within the prison system.

Consider the impact prison had on distance runner Johnny Gill. According to a 2003 story in the *Miami Herald*, Johnny had developed an excessive drinking problem that ultimately resulted in his committing armed robberies for which he was tried, found guilty, and sent to serve nearly seventy months in Oregon's Santiam Correctional Institution. When he started serving his term, the young prisoner's anger, bitterness, and fear drove him to fight with other inmates and to argue with guards. About a year into his sentence, Johnny's behavior earned him four months in **solitary confinement**, which turned out to be the **catalyst** for Johnny's change.

While in solitary, Johnny had time to think about his life—where he had been, what he had done, what he wanted to do next. He'd been a runner once, a good one with promise, and he had even moved to Oregon to train with veteran Olympic coach Dick Brown. But he'd drowned his chances to be an Olympian in alcohol and crime. Or had he?

Sitting alone in his cell, Johnny decided he had a choice: he could continue his self-destructive ways in and out of prison—or he could commit

FOUR PRIMARY PURPOSES OF IMPRISONMENT

- Punishment: to punish a convict by removing his freedom
- Public Protection: to protect the public from criminals and their crimes
- Deterrent: to discourage criminal behavior in others for fear of incarceration
- Rehabilitation: to help convicts become responsible, productive, and law-abiding

to becoming sober and to becoming the runner he hoped he could be. He made up his mind to take the second course of action, and he began training then and there in his solitary confinement cell. After completing his time in solitary, Johnny trained hard and became a model prisoner for the next four years until he finished his sentence. On his release in August 2003, Johnny moved in with his Olympic coach to begin training for the 2004 Olympic Track and Field Trials.

The thirty-four-year-old athlete summarized his attitude at the close of the *Miami Herald* article: "If you give your best effort and you know for years you've trained properly and done all the little things . . . and you still don't make it? So be it. . . . Hey, you gave it your best shot."

That attitude differed remarkably from the attitude of the angry young man Gill was when he entered prison. His incarceration resulted in positive change. Instead of living a life of alcohol-induced criminal behavior,

No two prisons are exactly the same.

Johnny Gill learned to give life his best shot. In the process, he found self-respect and purpose—two keys to successfully adjusting to post-prison life. Johnny had been rehabilitated.

Not all inmates in America's prisons see positive outcomes from their experiences as Johnny did. Some come out of prison more hardened and more bent on living a crime-filled life than ever before. What's the difference? Not all prisons are the same. No two prisoners or their experiences are alike. The differences between incarceration facilities, their populations, policies, and rehabilitation programs can make the difference between which prisoners "make it" and which ones don't.

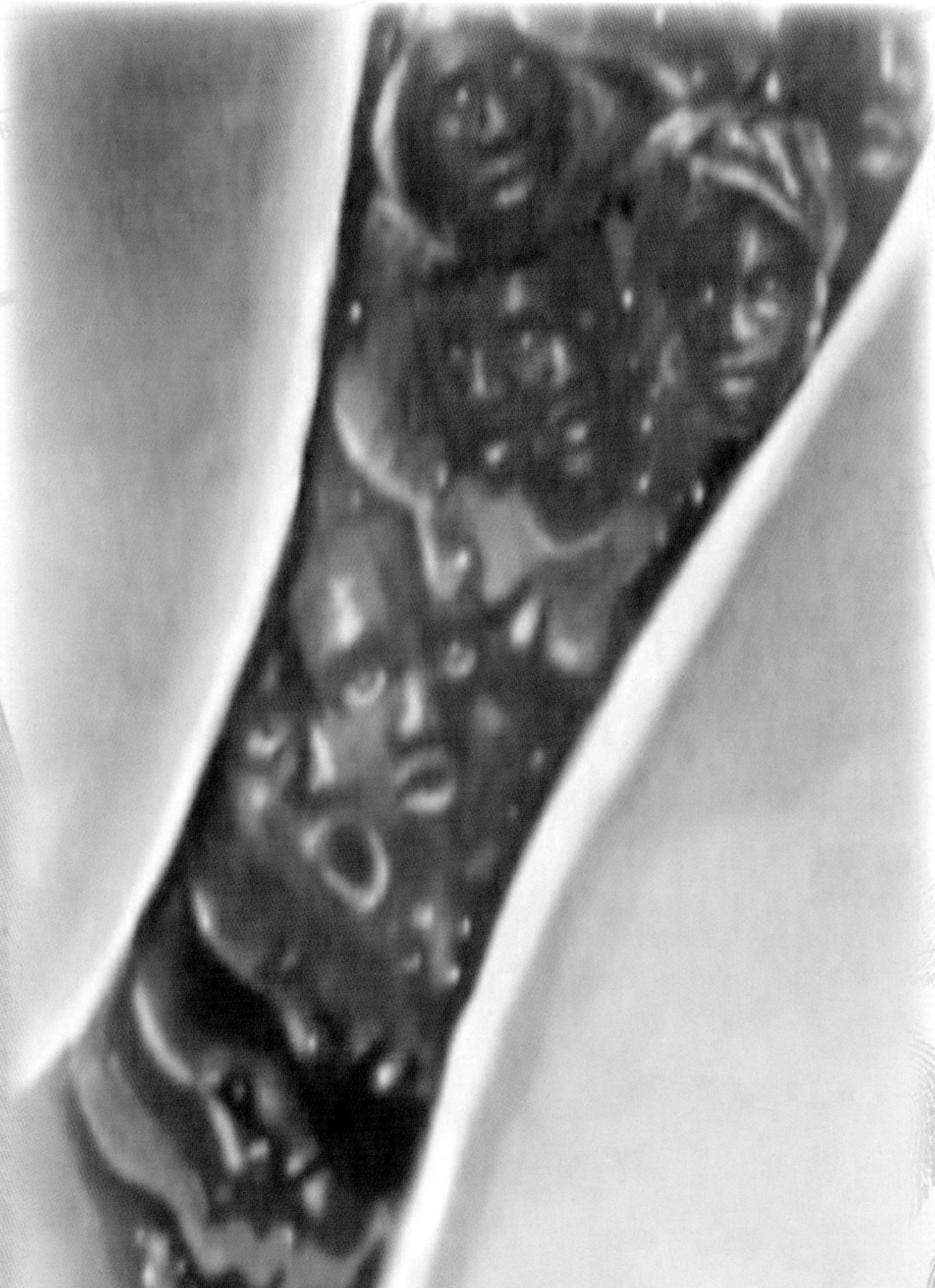

CHAPTER 2

DIFFERENT PRISONS, DIFFERENT EXPERIENCES: LEARNING TO ADJUST IS KEY

At the old McNeil Island . . . eight men and one toilet inhabited barred, open-tiered cells that were considerably smaller than the average household's living room. The cells were stacked four high, four deep, and four across, and they were situated in a filthy, drafty, nineteenth-century monster of a building that my students [the convicts] insisted, to a man, was haunted by many ghosts. One day, after a guard had given me a quick tour of the cell house on my way to class, I asked a student how he managed to survive in such a place.

"Always carry violence in your back pocket," he said, meaning, I presumed, that that was the best way and maybe the only method for avoiding [stabbings] and rapes.

"But how do you keep from going crazy?"

The student shrugged and said nothing, though perhaps his tight, scrunched-up body, his ever-darting eyes, and his tendency to get up and pace five or six times an hour had been giving me the answer all along.

—writing instructor Robert Ellis Gordon describing one of Washington State's correctional facilities in *The Funhouse Mirror: Reflections on Prison*

It's a prison, yeah, for kids. Everyone seventeen or younger. And they have security there, but there were freedoms we didn't have at that first jail, the one in the city. Here we had radios in the rooms, and we could play football and basketball and stuff. And there was a game room, with cards and Monopoly and games like that to play.

—seventeen-year-old "Mania" describing his first experience in a prison for juvenile offenders in *Teens in Prison* by Gail B. Stewart

*My cell measured about six feet by twelve with a ten-foot-high ceiling, from which dangled a single lightbulb with a pull chain. For furniture, I had a flat, hard steel bed and a steel desk and chair which had been assembled as one unit. The mandatory toilet afforded a sink directly above it with a steel medicine cabinet above that. High over the toilet was a rusty radiator, my only source of heat in the winter. Finally I had a flimsy wooden footlocker with a **hasp** that could be locked with a commissary-bought combination lock. My entrance was a solid steel sliding door with a fixed glass window on the top quarter. On the opposite wall was a window that could be manually opened and closed, just a little. The concrete walls were painted a dingy off-white and adorned with graffiti and cigarette stains.*

I began sleeping twelve to fourteen hours a day. My whole life consisted of eating, working, and sleeping. I never dreamed. I only tried to stay unconscious for as long as I possibly could. . . . In Graterford, a man who spends too much time in bed sends the same signal as that of a bleeding fish in shark-infested waters.

PRISONER REHABILITATION

Each prisoner's experience will be different.

The sign outside "Camp Cupcake," where Martha Stewart spent time.

"You can't be sleeping all the time," cautioned my chess partner one day, waking me to play a game. *"You can't sleep away your sentence. You have to stay awake to stay alive in here."*

—Victor Hassine, who began serving his life without the possibility of parole sentence in 1981 at Graterford State Prison in Pennsylvania, as quoted in *Doing Time: 25 Years of Prison Writing*

These quotes come from convicts serving time at incarceration facilities in the United States. One prisoner shares an open-barred cell with eight other convicts in a dark, stone structure built in the 1800s. Another lives with one roommate in a dormitory-style room in a bright, white-walled facility that looks more like a school than a prison. The third lives alone in a room with solid walls and a solid door. Courts convicted all three to confinement, yet their experiences differ vastly from one another's. And their experiences differ even more from that of media-mogul-turned-convict Martha Stewart.

Unlike Victor Hassine, whose sleepiness at Graterford State Prison could have cost him his life, Stewart didn't have to worry about whether she'd survive her ten-month sentence for conspiracy, obstruction, and two counts of lying to investigators about a stock trading deal. She served her time at a minimum-security federal correctional facility for women in rural West Virginia, a prison known by area residents as "Camp Cupcake" because of how easy it is to serve time there. Her prison-mates were primarily drug offenders doing time for possessing or using illegal drugs. Her "cellies" weren't murderers, serial killers, and rapists like those who lived with Hassine in Graterford, which instead of "Camp Cupcake" is known as "The Fort" and "Dodge City" because of its violent past.

In a September 2004 Associated Press (AP) article discussing Stewart's sentencing, a former employee of the Federal Correctional Institute of Alderson, West Virginia, where Stewart served her time, described the facility this way: "[The prison] looks a lot like a college. It's a beautiful campus." Another AP article in the same series described Stewart's prison home-away-from-home as being "set on a hill in a rural area. There are no metal fences surrounding the camp. Inmates have fixed schedules and

The cafeteria in a county jail has lower security than most federal prisons would.

must work, but free time can be spent playing volleyball, softball or tennis or doing aerobics." Fellow inmates told reporters that Stewart sometimes collected crabapples from trees on the prisons grounds where she walked and spent much of her free time learning to improve various microwave cooking methods, since microwave cooking was the only cooking method available to prisoners.

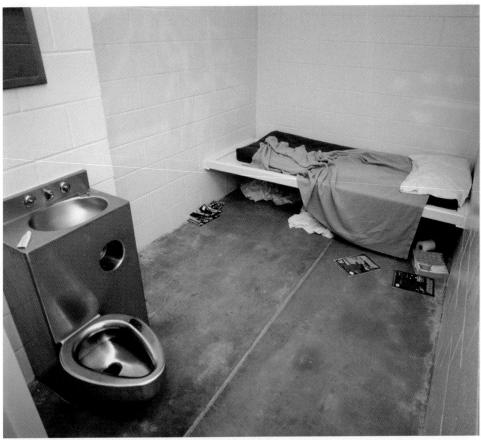
Many factors may influence where a female prisoner is held.

Two prisons; two convicts; two sentences: One convict wonders if he can stay alive; the other wonders if she can improve microwave recipes. How can two prison experiences be so different? As we noted in chapter 1, a convict's experience in prison depends on many things:

What crime did she commit?
Did she use violence?
Was anyone hurt in the commission of her crime?
How long is her sentence?
How old is she?
How big is she (physically)?
How attractive or unattractive is she?

DIFFERENT PRISONS, DIFFERENT EXPERIENCES

The sentencing judge decides the level of security warranted by the prisoner's crime.

How much education does she have?
Does she have a criminal record?
Is she a "frequent flyer" (repeat offender)?
What kind of attitude does she have?
Does she have any health (mental or physical) issues?
Where will she serve her time?

The sentencing judge uses most of these factors to determine which facility and level of security is best suited to the particular convict and her crime. Once the convict arrives at her incarceration facility, fellow inmates will use the same factors to size her up and determine where she

THE CONVICT'S HONOR RANKING OF CRIMINAL OFFENSES

Convicts have their own code of honor based on the nature of the offense for which an inmate is convicted. Some crimes earn immediate and high respect (a combination of reverence and fear). Others put an inmate on the bottom of the pecking order, making him an almost immediate target for abuse. Here's a sampling of crimes ranked from highest to lowest in amount of respect bestowed on the convict:

1. murder in the first degree (highest respect)
2. any other type of murder
3. any type of assault or attempted murder
4. armed robbery, especially of banks
5. kidnapping (without sexual assault involved)
6. drugs (any kind of drug-related offense)
7. various other crimes

LAST on the list: sexual crimes (rape, sodomy, sexual assault or abuse, etc.), especially against children. These crimes are so abhorred by other prisoners that they not only ensure the inmate will receive no respect, but they also make the convict a target for violence.

A prisoner who obeys the rules will have a better experience than one who doesn't—but his time incarcerated is still likely to be dismal and difficult.

fits in the prison social order. But the very same things that commended the convict to the judge may work against her with the prison population. Young, small, attractive, nonviolent, first-time inmates often become targeted by seasoned inmates for sexual advances and assault, as do those convicted for child molestation or rape. Older convicts, tough-looking newcomers, and repeat offenders, especially those committed to prison for murder, are given more respect and distance. No one messes with them.

Once other prisoners make these determinations, the new inmate's experiences with other prisoners and guards depends primarily on two other things: how well she follows prison rules and how well she follows the convict code (see sidebar).

Every prison provides a handbook to each prisoner at his orientation that outlines the basics of daily life: his daily schedule, when he can

THE CONVICT CODE

Within every prison, convicts hold to an unspoken, universal code of behavior that if followed can help them survive prison without much harm. If they violate the unspoken code, they can expect to become the victims of violence or assault. Authors Jeffrey Ian Ross and Stephen C. Richards in their book *Behind Bars: Surviving Prison* describe the code this way:

Do:
Mind your own business.
Watch what you say.
Be loyal to convicts as a group.
Play it cool.
Be sharp.
Be honorable.
Do your own time.
Be tough.
Be a man.
Pay your debts.

Don't:
Snitch on another convict.
Pressure another convict.
Lose your head.
Attract attention.
Exploit other convicts.
Break your word.

A prison library, where inmates may read or study.

shower, when he can eat, where he can eat, how to get his food, where to take his dirty linens, how to get clean laundry, what he can and cannot have in his cell or dormitory, what he can and cannot wear, what he can buy at the prison store or commissary, when he can use the phone, when and if he can leave his cell, when and if he can go outside, when and if he can use the prison library, when he can go to the infirmary, how to obtain medical treatment, how to obtain new clothing when needed, how to mail letters or receive visitors, when he can receive a hug from a visitor and for how long, how to make contact with his lawyer, other basic rules of conduct, and basic consequences to violating the rules. Some rules found in the prison handbook would be statements like: "always obey a direct order," "always stand for head counts," "report to your assigned job on time," "no fighting allowed," "no weapons allowed," "no drugs al-

Prisoners often respond well to animals rescued from shelters.

lowed," "no screaming," "quiet after lights out," "guards have the right to search you or your cell at any time without notice."

The better an inmate follows the rules, the more likely his prison experience will be positive. He may be rewarded with better-paying jobs ($0.40 per hour instead of $0.10 per hour) or greater responsibility (move from serving food in the chow line, for example, to working as a file clerk). He may earn time off of his sentence for good behavior, meaning that he might be released from prison early or become eligible for **parole** because he's stayed out trouble while serving his time. Most important, following the rules might make a convict eligible for the various rehabilitation programs offered within the facility.

Rehabilitation programs can include everything from reading programs to high school equivalency classes, for-credit college courses to vocational or technical job skills training, counseling and anger-management classes to drug rehabilitation programs. Some prisons include animal-training programs where inmates teach dogs basic obedience skills to prepare the animals for service as guide dogs for people with blindness or as aid dogs for people with physical or motor challenges. Other animal-training programs serve as animal rescues by taking animals from shelters where they were scheduled for *euthanasia* and giving them to prisoners who teach them basic obedience commands to make the animals fit for adoption by loving families. We'll discuss the details of several rehabilitation programs in later chapters, but a prisoner's ability to adjust to prison life and follow prison rules determines whether or not he is chosen to participate in these programs.

Though different prisons have different rules, inmates help themselves by learning the ropes quickly. The official prison rules for prisoner conduct issued by prison officials aren't the only ones convicts need to learn to foster a positive prison experience; they have to follow the convict code as well—a series of unspoken, though agreed-upon, rules of behavior established by inmates and expected of inmates by other inmates. It isn't enough to follow prison rules; an inmate has to follow inmate rules as well.

Breaking the convict code in any jail, prison, or detention center can have serious consequences including anything from banishment from certain groups or gangs to sudden, often violent death. Prisoners will use physical assaults, threats, and rape to enforce the convict code, including its lesser offenses. Of all the rules in the code, the rule against informing on other inmates is the most seriously enforced. Snitches—those who tell on other inmates—can wind up dead in the middle of a crowded cell block without another soul admitting to seeing a thing.

Life in prison isn't easy, but learning to follow the rules, both the prison rules and the convict code, can go a long way toward helping an inmate survive her experience. She may not only survive; she can actually grow and change—become rehabilitated—if she takes advantage of

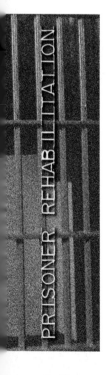

THE CONVICT CODE, ANOTHER VERSION

Former inmate T. J. Granack, currently paroled from a fifteen-to-thirty-year sentence and working as a bartender, offers this advice, similar to the Convict Code, in his article "Welcome to the Steel Hotel: Survival Tips for Beginners," in *The Funhouse Mirror: Reflections on Prison* by Robert Ellis Gordon and Inmates (current or former) of the Washington Corrections system:

1. Commit an honorable crime (murder, not sexual molestation, for example).
2. Don't gamble.
3. Be poor.
4. Never loan anyone anything.
5. Buy cigarettes (whether you smoke or not).
6. Make no eye contact.
7. Pick your friends carefully.
8. Fight and fight dirty.
9. Be ugly.
10. Mind your own business.
11. Don't talk to staff, especially guards.
12. Never snitch.

Many prisoners end up returning to prison after they are released.

the learning privileges, job-training classes, and various prison service programs or clubs made available to her as she adjusts to prison life. She can, in these instances, choose to use her prison time to better herself. Not all inmates do. The choice to use prison time constructively can make a huge difference in how positive an inmate's prison experience will be and whether or not that prisoner becomes rehabilitated.

The prison system in North America (both in Canada and the United States) is by no means perfect. And learning to adjust to prison life can't always guarantee a positive prison experience. But many prisons offer programs that give inmates hope for rehabilitation and greater self-respect. The best prison programs and methods result in positive, life-altering outcomes for convicts. Their inmates become success stories of rehabilitation.

Not all convicts, however, end up with positive life outcomes. Not every convict is rehabilitated. Many return to lives of crime or violence. These are what society calls "hardened" criminals. Sometimes these individuals have a psychological disorder that causes them to act as they do, and no amount of prison time or anger-management training will help them change. But others remain unchanged because they've fallen prey to the dark side of prison—things that can destructively influence inmates and prevent their successful rehabilitation: prison violence, gang affiliations, inequality in prisoner treatment; faulty sentencing guidelines that result in unfair sentences; a prison drug subculture and rampant prisoner drug abuse; a shortage of proper drug treatment facilities; lack of educational opportunities in some facilities; corruption among prison officials; overcrowding; housing violent inmates with nonviolent inmates. Researchers document that these things contribute to high *recidivism* rates and increasingly violent behaviors in prisons and jails.

Yet even in face of these difficult issues, some prisoners are successfully rehabilitated. Sometimes the difference is the character of the prisoners themselves (beliefs, values, motivation, etc.); sometimes the difference is their ability to adjust to prison life; sometimes the difference is the quality and availability of prison programs. And sometimes it's how the prisoner and the prison system in which he finds himself view the process of rehabilitation itself.

DIFFERENT PRISONS, DIFFERENT EXPERIENCES

DATE
9-28-00

EMPLOYER AND ADDRESS

SOCIAL SECURITY

DRIVER'S LIC. NO. TO STATE

REASON FINGER

PRISONER REHABILITATION

42

CHAPTER 3

REHABILITATION: THREE PROGRAMS THAT WORK

"We must accept the reality that to confine offenders behind walls without trying to change them is an expensive folly with short-term benefits—winning battles while losing the war."

—former U.S. Supreme Court Justice Warren Burger

Education is part of many rehabilitation programs.

Class began at 8:30 A.M. sharp. Fifteen students sat attentively in molded plastic chairs with their notepads, pencils, and calculators splayed across the writing surfaces the chairs' desk-arms provided. The wire racks beneath their seats served more as footrests or heel props than book holders, but that made the undersized chairs more comfortable for the students squeezed between their writing surfaces and seats. The instructor warmly greeted her students and started the morning session by talking about how to determine the value of a used car. After a brief explanation of looking up "blue book" values for used vehicles and what things to look for to determine a car's condition, the teacher distributed a series of handouts. The assignment? To figure out how much they should offer to pay for the car described in their handouts and whether or not they could afford that price based on what their monthly payments would be if they took out a loan for the price of the car and repaid the loan over four years.

Like students in many classes, some immediately went to work punching calculator keys and individually scribbling their calculations while others worked in groups to come up with a fair negotiating price and reasonable repayment plan. A few students raised their hands and asked for help. Some seemed lost, but attempted to do the work anyway. The teacher circulated among the students and offered help as needed. All worked hard at completing the assignment.

After giving them time to work on their own, the teacher asked one pupil to go to the chalkboard and write down how she figured out the price for the car. If the student at the board got stuck with any step of the problem, others in the class helped her. Another student then went to the board to show her calculations for another part of the problem. The lively banter between students displayed their growing understanding of the process involved in buying and financing a used car. Then class time was over.

The first class ended at 9:30 A.M.; the second began fifteen minutes later. Instead of learning how to do percentages and multiplication, the students in this class gave oral presentations on the topic "trading spaces." Each student was asked to identify one person—any person—

Most minimum- and moderate-security facilities have classrooms inside them.

with whom they'd like to temporarily switch lives and then to explain why. Instead of completing a writing assignment, these students had to stand in front of the class and talk about who they chose and what made them choose that person. By making them think about what they wanted in life, this assignment helped students identify what really mattered to them. By speaking in front of the class, the students were learning how to present themselves to others.

These classes sound like they could be high school math and language arts classes, don't they? In fact, they are life skills classes taught by Isabel Companiony at Delores J. Baylor Women's Correctional Institution in New Castle, Delaware. The students are inmates.

According to the U.S. National Institute of Justice (NIJ), the Delaware Department of Correction offers a four-month life skills program in four state prisons twice a year. Up to 150 minimum-security and medium-security inmates participate in the program each time, attending structured

WHAT IS MRT?

Moral Reconation Therapy (MRT) is the central component to life skills programs like that used in Delaware. It's a step-by-step method that helps students change the way they *act* by changing the way they *think*. Using reflective exercises, assignments, and group discussions, MRT enables participants to better identify and assess their feelings, thoughts, experiences, values, and relationships, and then helps them handle these areas in healthier ways. Some themes in MRT include caring for others, being honest, and taking responsibility.

MRT also requires students to plan for their futures. Students must set realistic goals for when they leave prison—where they want to be one year from now, two years from now, five years from now, etc.—and figure out how to achieve their goals using law-abiding practices. One final MRT requirement is completing twenty hours of volunteer work.

classes for four months, Mondays through Fridays, three hours per day. The courses cover academics (reading, math, language), violence reduction (Moral Reconation Therapy [MRT], anger management, conflict resolution), and the skills necessary to make it in daily life (credit management and banking, finding and keeping a job, motor vehicle regulations, family responsibilities, legal responsibilities, health issues). Nearly three hundred inmates enroll in these classes each year, 85 percent of whom successfully complete the program's graduation requirements.

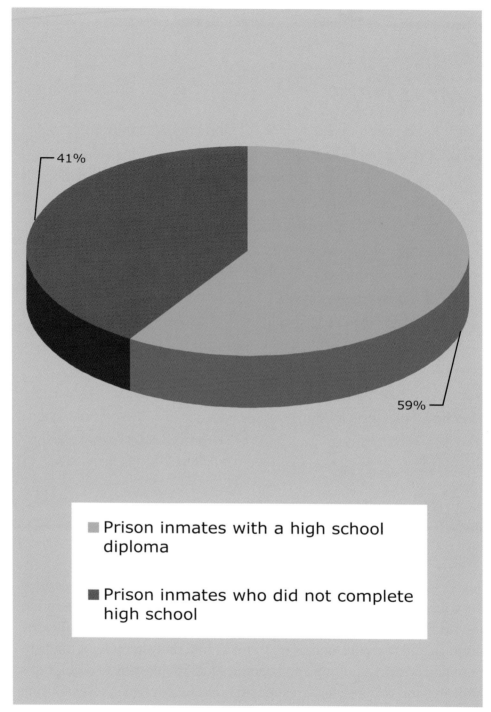

41%

59%

Prison inmates with a high school diploma

Prison inmates who did not complete high school

A little more than 40 percent of all inmates in the United States never completed high school.

Prisoners who are released with better reading and writing skills will have an increased likelihood of supporting themselves without resorting to crime.

Life skills programs like these target inmates who are scheduled for release soon after the courses are scheduled to end. They attempt to help students learn what they need to successfully transition to life outside prison walls.

The idea of educating prisoners is nothing new. A special report by the Bureau of Justice Statistics cited that in 1997, roughly 41 percent of inmates in U.S. prisons had not completed high school or its equivalent. That statistic remained the same for most of the 1990s. In Canada, the National Crime Prevention Centre cites that statistic to be closer to 37 percent for Canadian inmates. For decades, prison officials across North America have known that basic education is necessary for transition from prison to success in ordinary life. To address this need, nine out of ten state prisons in the United States offer educational programs for inmates: high school equivalency classes, GED (general educational development) classes, adult basic education (ABE) classes, college courses, or vocational and certificate programs. What prison officials and

Basic computer skills are essential for success in today's world.

ONE TEACHER'S PERSPECTIVE

The teachers in life skills programs integrate MRT with other subjects like banking or English literature. When teaching on managing credit, for example, a teacher will challenge students about the rightness or wrongness of not paying off credit card debt. When reading about characters in literature, the teacher may have the students rate characters according to a morality scale. The point of MRT, as one life skills teacher put it, "is to challenge [the students'] belief system repeatedly so they begin to think in terms of what is the right thing to do."

sociologists are discovering, however, is that inmates need more than the ability to read and write to make it in the real world; they need other skills, too, like how to control their anger, how to find a job, and how to make and sustain healthy relationships. That's what makes Delaware's program (and similar programs across North America) so effective. These programs integrate relationship skills, *values determination*, and emotions management (mostly learned through MRT) with other life skills classes and academics.

To date, the U.S. Department of Education's Office of Correctional Education has funded eighteen life skills programs nationwide. Analysis done by NIJ researchers concluded that inmates who participated in the life skills progams (that included MRT) exhibited fewer problem behaviors while in prison and less incidents of returning to criminal behavior when released. MRT-integrated life skills training seemed to work.

Food services is a useful skill for prisoners to learn.

Students seem to value MRT. One former student and life skills graduate expressed it this way:

> The MRT steps helped me most in life skills, beginning with the first step of honesty. That step is as clear in my mind today as if I just read it. I always felt stealing, lying—politicians and preachers do it, so why not me? But I learned to do the right thing. Now I work for an employer who trusts me with the keys to his house.

The idea behind prison life skills training programs is that by giving inmates all the tools they need to succeed in key spheres of life (relationships, jobs, feelings management, and values like honesty and integrity), prisons are helping inmates to become productive, law-abiding citizens.

If you define rehabilitation as turning a convict from her life of crime, programs like the one in Delaware could be said to successfully rehabilitate convicts. One study tracked Delaware's program graduates for two years after their release from prison. Of the twenty female prisoners who completed the life skills program, only three (15 percent) had been charged with or convicted of new crimes within two years of their release, compared to nearly 51 percent of the females who were released but did not take life skills training. In one of Delaware's men's prisons, only nine of forty (23 percent) life skills graduates were charged with or convicted of new crimes within two years of their release, while ten of twenty released men (50 percent) who did not complete life skills wound up behind bars again.

Several life skills training programs that use MRT are helping prisoners change in America, but they aren't the only methods that successfully rehabilitate convicted criminals. Consider Canada's CORCAN program.

CORCAN (short for Corrections Canada) is the Correctional Service of Canada's (CSC) primary rehabilitation program. It offers over two million hours of employment training and employability skills training to convicts in Canada's federal prison system each year. According to the CSC, over 5,000 federally sentenced imprisoned convicts work in CORCAN positions annually at thirty-one sites across Canada. These positions provide inmates with training for jobs in textiles, *agribusiness*, manufacturing, construction, and maintenances services. CORCAN employees build furniture, produce food, work on construction projects, manufacture clothing, clean parks and recreational areas, build or refurbish homes for the homeless, provide laundry services, and work in printing and scanning services—all while serving their time behind bars.

CORCAN also employs 1,900 offenders annually who are no longer in prison but living in communities while under *supervised release* from prison or out on parole. CORAN helps inmates transition from jobs on the inside to jobs on the outside by offering employment counseling on release. CORCAN's employment counseling offices help inmates by evaluating their employability (attitudes, work habits, skills, training needs, interviewing skills), helping them search for jobs and to write resumes,

Watching television is a privilege prisoners can earn with good behavior.

developing company partnerships by which companies agree to hire former offenders, and by offering ongoing support.

Inmates working in CORCAN shops experience working environments similar to what they'd find in the real world, and they are expected to behave as they would if they held the same job on their release from prison: they must treat others with courtesy and respect; they have to arrive for work on time; they have to put in a full day's work; they have to meet deadlines, production targets, and sales goals; they have to know how to take constructive criticism; they have to take on and manage responsibility; they have to maintain the skills necessary to perform their jobs; they have to display honesty and commitment. CORCAN supervisors believe that the more realistic the work experience is for the offender, the more effective the experience will be in rehabilitating the prisoner.

So far, their position seems accurate. CORCAN states that it saw a nearly 30 percent reduction in re-offenses (returning to crime) for paroled convicts who worked in CORCAN jobs in 1996. CORCAN appears to be helping Canadian offenders turn their lives around.

Another program, this one located on the southern end of North America, is helping American offenders to do the same. The Orange County, Florida, Jail Educational and Vocational Program includes MRT and life skills training like that used in Delaware's prisons *and* vocational training similar to that used in Canada—but it adds two other components that seem to make a substantial difference in inmates lives.

> I didn't want to participate in any programs, but that was the only way I could get . . . into one of the buildings that have open spaces, only two guys to a cell, and good visitation rights. So I wouldn't have taken MRT if I didn't have to, but I'm glad I did. I learned about myself. . . . In life skills classes, I learned how to write a resume and present myself at a job interview, like sitting up straight. But you have to obey the rules in the program facilities if you want to stay. I've seen guys get busted back [to other facilities] because of shouting matches between inmates. A few come back here again, but then they're careful to behave, because the other facility stinks. There's loud noise that keeps you from sleeping, it's cold, and there's no carpeting, so they like it here much better.

At first you might think this inmate was describing the program in a Delaware state prison. But this quote comes from an inmate in the Orange County jail who was quoted in the NIJ's *Program Focus* bulletin on the Orange County, Florida, Jail Educational and Vocational Program. If you look closely at the quote, you'll see one difference: in addition to MRT, life skills, and job training, Orange County adds a rewards system to the rehabilitation mix. If inmates in Orange County jails participate in programs and stay out of trouble, they can earn valuable privileges like nicer housing, better visitation policies, library services, televisions, and

REHABILITATION

newspaper subscriptions. In short, by participating in the education and vocational programs and obeying the rules, Orange County inmates not only receive much of what they need to successfully move into jobs outside prison walls, they also improve their quality of life on the inside.

While training (educational and vocational) is an important part of Orange County's approach to rehabilitation, as it is in Delaware and Canada, it is only one part of a three-part process. If you imagined a three-legged stool, education and job training would be only one leg supporting the stool; direct supervision and behavioral incentives are the other two legs.

Direct supervision is a process by which many of the physical barriers between inmates and staff are removed (things like bars, glass, metal doors). The buildings are designed to foster more direct contact between those who live in the building and those who work there and to give inmates more freedom to move about the facility. It makes the inmates feel more human and facilitates better interactions between inmates and staff.

Buildings designed for direct supervision programs use ordinary commercial furniture (like you might see in a public library), normal plumbing fixtures (instead of bolted-down stainless steel), and average-security hardware (like door locks instead of metal bars). Each building typically contains two or more self-contained sections called "pods" that hold several two-person rooms (inmate cells) opening onto a spacious common area used as a classroom and day room manned by a single officer at a desk. The inmates can freely come and go between their rooms and the open area throughout the day. Only one or two guards watch the pod, and they circulate as needed.

Because the inmates have so much direct contact with their supervisors, it's difficult to hide misbehavior. That's where behavioral incentives come into play. Some incentives involve avoiding negative consequences. Prison staff, for example, can send an inmate back to basic housing at any time for misconduct like chronically being late for class or shouting at other inmates. Other incentives offer positive rewards. In Florida, most sentenced inmates can earn five days of gain time (five days taken off their sentence total) for every month they follow the rules.

ORANGE COUNTY'S JAIL OPTIONS

If you cause trouble, are expected to remain in jail for sixty days or less, require maximum security, refuse to participate in programs, or are mentally ill, you are assigned to live in Orange County's basic housing facility. If you choose to participate in the educational and vocational programs, you can stay in a program facility that offers many amenities.

In basic housing you receive these privileges:

- limited visits and telephone use (no contact)
- limited recreation activities (three hours per week)
- limited prison store privileges

In the educational and vocational progam facilities you receive the following privileges:

- visits and telephone use
- recreation activities
- prison store privileges
- library services
- newspapers
- secure personal lockers
- additional gain time (a way to reduce your sentence length)
- television
- contact visits (you can touch and hug your visitors)
- the option for coed housing
- nondormitory living, two people per room
- air conditioning
- carpeting
- direct supervision (maximum contact between staff and inmates without physical barriers in between)

Auto maintenance is just one type of vocational training prisoners can learn.

In Orange County, if you participate in the educational and vocational training programs, you can earn an additional six days of gain time (for a total of eleven days) for every month you participate and follow the rules. Good behavior plus program participation equals less time in jail.

Florida officials state that less than 5 percent of Orange County inmates refuse to participate in its programs, and that's due largely to the incentives attached to program participation.

Because they receive direct supervision and behavioral incentives, most of Orange County's participating inmates are motivated students. Orange County Jail offers five types of courses: basic education (ABE, GED, remedial reading, English as a second language, basic literacy); vocational training (auto maintenance, desktop publishing, carpentry, culinary arts, electrical wiring); life skills programs (job skills, job search strategies, parenting, relationship skills, money management); psycho-educational support groups for women (counseling in self-esteem, maintaining sobriety, anger management); and substance abuse education (including MRT). Inmates enrolled in the program may join any class already in progress as long as space permits. If they took all that was available to them (and some do), inmates could be in classes as much as nine hours per day. Basic education, vocational training, and life skills all require six hours of classes five days per week. Support groups and substance abuse education require additional time. The required time investment to participate gives inmates more ownership of the program and keeps them busy—something that leads to reduced disturbances and less conflict among those living in Orange County's program facilities.

Orange County, Florida. The state of Delaware. The nation of Canada. Rehabilitation programs are working in all three places. Prison officials in these arenas view rehabilitation as a **proactive** responsibility of the correctional system as well as the duty of an inmate, and they see it as more than just involving job training or education alone. They've taken comprehensive approaches that include nurturing the hearts (values, beliefs, and ethics), minds (education), and hands (skill training) of criminals to turn them into responsible citizens. As one prison official put it, they change "tax takers" into "taxpayers." And many graduates of these programs go on to lead productive, responsible lives. To do so, they have to not only successfully navigate the system's rehabilitation programs *in* prison, but they have to learn to adjust to life outside their prison walls.

60

CHAPTER 4

Transitioning to Life Outside the Walls

After I'd served two years in prison, I hooked up with [an employment specialist] because my parole officer referred me specifically to him. . . . In two weeks [he] got me a job as a machine presser, and I was trained on the job. I couldn't land one on my own—I filled out applications, but no one would hire me. [The employment specialist] also got me into an eight-month welding course, which will begin in six months, that I can do while I'm still working.

This quote, from a former inmate in Chicago, reveals one major barrier former inmates face when they leave prison and enter the real world: finding people to hire them. Chicago's Safer Foundation is working hard to remedy that problem.

Founded in 1972, the Safer Foundation is the United States' largest community-based employment services provider for ex-offenders. Safer Foundation literature describes its role in helping ex-offenders:

> The Safer Foundation is a private non-profit organization that helps ex-offenders help themselves stay out of prison and turn their lives around. We believe that keeping a job is the best way to do this, and all of our programs are aimed at that goal. We work only with offenders—so we understand the problems they face in finding and keeping a job.

A former Safer Foundation participant's story illustrates how the Safer Foundation works (this story is adapted from and recorded in more detail in the NIJ's National Institute of Corrections' Office of Correctional Education's Program Focus publication *Chicago's Safer Foundation: A Road Back for Ex-Offenders*):

> Six-feet, one-inch, 210 pounds, and in his early twenties, Doug came to [Safer's work release facility] brimming with anger and a jaded "seen it all, done it all" attitude. Before going to prison for assault and battery, Doug had been an ***incorrigible*** foster child and an active gang member. Guided by his [work release] case manager, Doug received his GED in the Safer basic education program . . . and enrolled in a local vocational school to study culinary arts. [A Safer facility] supervisor mentored Doug, helping him keep his hostility in check. After his release, Doug continued his schooling at the vocational school. . . . Doug is now the head chef in an upscale Chicago restaurant.

Because of Safer's investment in supporting Doug from work release through his education and into the work world, Doug made a successful transition from prison to community life. His reentry is complete.

Reentry (or "reintegration," as it's called in Canada) is the new buzzword in criminal justice circles. "Reentry" describes the process of inmates

PRISONER REHABILITATION

Thanks to the Safer Foundation, ex-offenders can create entire new lives for themselves.

leaving prisons and jails and reentering the neighborhoods and communities around them. According to the U.S. Bureau of Justice Statistics, at least 95 percent of all state prisoners in the United States will be released from prison at some point in their sentences. In 2001 alone, 592,000 state prison inmates were released. By the end of 2002, over 670,000 adult former inmates were living in American communities while under state parole. In 2003, if you include adult men and women under federal, state, and local probation or parole, that number increases to 4.8 *million*! The Sentencing Project, a nonprofit organization based in Washington, D.C., estimates that nearly 1,600 inmates are released from prison in America each day, one-third of whom are ex-drug offenders and one-fourth of whom are ex-violent offenders.

What are communities supposed to do with these returning members of society?

One important step communities can make is the realization that if released inmates are to transition successfully from incarceration to freedom, they need support in prison, on release, and for months afterward. Ward Thurman, who served four years of a forty-year sentence (ten years suspended) for **mitigated** murder, summed up the challenge of reentering society in an article published by Prison Fellowship Ministries: "The first year was the most stressful. There were days I thought it would be easier to go back [to prison]." But as he reveals later in the article, this former inmate had something going for him that many ex-offenders don't: a **mentor**, someone who would meet with him and check up on him and support him through the transition. "He [Ward's mentor] came up every week and met me on campus, bought me a Coke, and we'd talk school, politics, life. I scheduled that time."

Ward's mentor also happened to be a retired professor with connections at a local technical school. With his help, Ward was accepted into a degree program and finished his bachelor's degree in less than five years. Today, fourteen years after his release, Ward has a good job as an overseer in the mining industry, something his degree in **metallurgy** helped him obtain, and he is happily married with three small sons. He remains arrest free and has even developed a reputation of integrity among those who know and work with him.

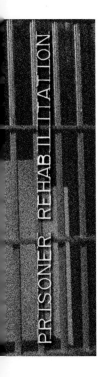

PRISONER REHABILITATION

PRISONER STATISTICS

Just who is being released from prison in recent years? The Bureau of Justice Statistics (BOJS) released these findings in its report *State and Federal Prisoners Returning to the Community: Findings from the Bureau of Justice Statistics* (April 13, 2000) based on figures from 1997 and 1998:

- 12 percent are female
- 21 percent are Hispanic
- 35 percent are middle-aged (between the ages of thirty-five and fifty-four)
- 35 percent were drug law violators
- 24 percent were violent offenders
- most served longer times in prison (averaging twenty-seven months)

Statistics for 2003 round out the picture (from the BOJS):

- nearly 50 percent had committed felonies
- 95 percent had been sentenced to serve more than one year
- 23 percent were women
- 56 percent of those on probation were white
- 30 percent of those on probation were black
- 12 percent of those on probation were Hispanic

Successful rehabilitation programs offer everything from vocational skills to high school equivalency courses.

Mentors can play an important role in helping ex-offenders find their places in society.

Without the support of a mentor, statistics indicate that neither Ward nor Doug (from the Safer Foundation) would have had much success at reentry. Apparently, personal support plays a large role in helping inmates transition to outside life. Personal support and job placement, though helpful, however, can't carry the load completely. Researchers have concluded that the most successful reentry outcomes happen when ex-offenders participate in a multistage transition.

In a report on a 2002 NIJ-sponsored project titled *From Prison Safety to Public Safety: Innovations in Offender Reentry*, researchers recommend that for a reentry process to work, it needs to involve three overlapping phases: the *institutional* phase, the *structured reentry* phase, and the *community reintegration* phase. The institutional phase includes that time when an offender is in prison. It would attempt to prepare the inmate for return to society from the minute she steps behind bars. Programs included during this first phase would be similar to what is offered in Delaware's state prisons, Florida's Orange County Jail, and Canada's

Churches and other faith-based institutions often play a role in an ex-offender's reentry into society.

vocational rehabilitation program (described in the previous chapter): educational services, job-training programs, life skills classes, appropriate treatment for substance abuse and mental illness. The idea is to prepare the inmate for release while she is still in custody.

The next phase, structured reentry, begins in prison when the inmate becomes eligible for release and continues through the first month (or longer) of her transition into the community. This part of the process ensures that on release the inmate can find adequate housing, food, transportation, and a legal means of income. This might be arranged through the inmate's family connections, halfway houses, various levels of parole, community-based group homes, ex-prisoner advocacy networks, work-release programs, or faith-based agencies.

Once the ex-inmate knows her basic needs will be met, the next phase kicks in: the community reintegration phase. According to NIJ researchers, this phase usually begins during the second month after re-

A SAMPLING OF ORGANIZATIONS DEDICATED TO PREPARING AND ASSISTING INMATES WITH REENTRY

CAEFS (Canadian Association of Elizabeth Fry Societies)
CORM (Conquest Offender Reintegration Ministries)
CURE (Citizens United for Rehabilitation of Errants)
Family and Corrections Network
John Howard Society of Canada
OPEN (Offender Preparation and Education Network, Inc.)
Prison Fellowship Ministries
Restorative Justice Ministry Network of North America

lease. The focus then becomes maintaining the gains the offender made in her first month of release, ensuring ongoing support and accountability, and moving her toward law-abiding self-sufficiency.

The best reentry results, this study maintains, occur when a partnership exists between the criminal justice system, social services, and the community at large that works to offer the support ex-inmates need to survive in the real world.

The U.S. Department of Justice's Office of Justice Programs (OJP) recently undertook an effort to promote this three-stage transition to communities in America by developing a comprehensive strategy to address the issue of ex-offenders returning home. Titled the Serious and Violent

Offender Reentry Initiative, the OJP's plan encourages implementation stages much like those the NIJ researchers recommended:

Phase 1: Protect and Prepare: Institution-Based Programs
Phase 2: Control and Restore: Community-Based Transition Programs
Phase 3: Sustain and Support: Community-Based Long-Term Support Programs

In April 2002, Virginia's Department of Corrections started a new program that closely resembles this three-phase approach. Started in Southside Regional Jail in Emporia, Virginia, this program focuses on preparing inmates for their return to civilian life by having select inmates work through three transition stages. In this case, Phase One is called Programming, during which for forty-five days before release, the inmate participates in daily workshops that cover topics including life skills, cognitive thinking, employability, conflict resolution, substance abuse, anger management, and domestic violence. Outside services also come into the jail to provide help with finding jobs and housing.

After the programming phase, the inmate moves into Phase Two: Work Release. During this transition stage, the inmate is released from prison to work a specific job, but is still supervised. When he completes this forty-five-day stage, he is then eligible for Phase Three: Community Release. During Community Release, these offenders have to take classes twice a week for another forty-five days, but they are out of prison and actively connected with community resources.

According to Virginia's Department of Corrections, this three-phase approach allows the offender to leave prison or jail with the life skills, job-training, and job search skills he needs to successfully transition into community life. If a former inmate can successfully transition to life outside of prison walls, his chances of becoming a rehabilitation success story dramatically improve.

Just what does it mean to be successfully rehabilitated? Ned Rollo, executive director of OPEN, Inc. ("Offender Preparation and Education Network" of Dallas, Texas), an organization whose stated mission is "to motivate and prepare persons with a criminal history to adopt and main-

PRISONER REHABILITATION

TYPES OF TRANSITIONAL RELEASES AND LIVING SITUATIONS

Transitional releases from incarceration are periods of time when offenders can leave their incarceration facilities to participate in jobs or activities in the community as part of their transition from prison life. These releases can range in length from just a few hours to days or weeks at a time. They are known by different names:

- temporary absences (TAs) (Canada)
- treatment release (release to a medical or mental health facility)
- work release (supervised work program outside of the facility)
- day parole (living in the incarceration facility, but released during the day)
- full parole (after imprisonment, serving part of a sentence while living in the community)
- halfway houses (community-based, supervised living facilities)
- statutory release (when laws require that an inmate serve part of his sentence in the community while under supervision)

tain a socially responsible and personally rewarding lifestyle," describes "success" for former offenders this way:

> Success for a person with a felony history is a dynamic condition of recognizable growth—a purposeful process of positive unfolding combined with an expanding sense of belonging and constructive participation. . . . [It] is a state of positive "becoming"—an evolution, out of the

Once an offender should not mean always an offender.

A PROGRAM THAT HELPS EX-OFFENDERS FIND JOBS

New York City's Center for Employment Opportunities (CEO) helps newly released offenders prepare for, find, and keep jobs. One week after release from incarceration, program participants are assigned to day-labor work crews. These crews allow workers to earn immediate cash, develop confidence and self-esteem by holding down a job seven hours per day, learn good work habits, and gain an accurate assessment of what will be expected of them in the workplace. Typical work crew assignments include custodial services for buildings, roadside cleanup and repair, park maintenance, groundskeeping, and other exterior work. To remain in the program, participants must strictly follow CEO rules about punctuality, dress code, work crew rules, and disciplinary procedures. Seventy percent of CEO program participants find full-time employment with other employers within two to three months of working for CEO.

ashes of past misdeeds, beyond the grip of sorrow, fear, shame and rage, into a deep appreciation for lessons learned, a commitment to make a rewarding contribution to others and a deep-seated gratitude for the nature and scope of one's life experience.

Rollo should know. He's an ex-offender who served five and a half years in state and federal prisons for manslaughter, drug possession, and

Does justice mean more than punishment? What does society owe offenders?

firearms violations. He is also a nationally recognized correctional training specialist with thirty-six years of experience in the corrections field, a career he started after his release from prison.

Former Chief Juvenile Probation Officer of Bucks County, Pennsylvania, William D. Ford, defines successful rehabilitation more **succinctly**, feeling that success has occurred when a former offender is working legitimately and staying clean. Ford considers an offender to be rehabilitated when "he's a taxpayer, is arrest free, and has made **restitution**," as he stated in a recent interview for this book. When asked what factors contributed most to successful rehabilitation, the former probation officer with forty-one years' experience with juvenile offenders didn't hesitate: "love, understanding, compassion, educational opportunities, nurturing, boundaries, and limitations." The primary key, he explained, is relationship.

Even with the best programs in place, even with comprehensive three-phase strategies, statistics indicate that offenders who leave incarceration without relational connection—without supportive friends, family, coworkers, or advocates on the outside—are more than likely to fail at their reentry attempts. Can anything be done to help these men, women, and teens?

DATE 9-28-00

EMPLOYER AND ADDRESS

REASON FINGE

SOCIAL SECURITY

MIDD

E. MIDS

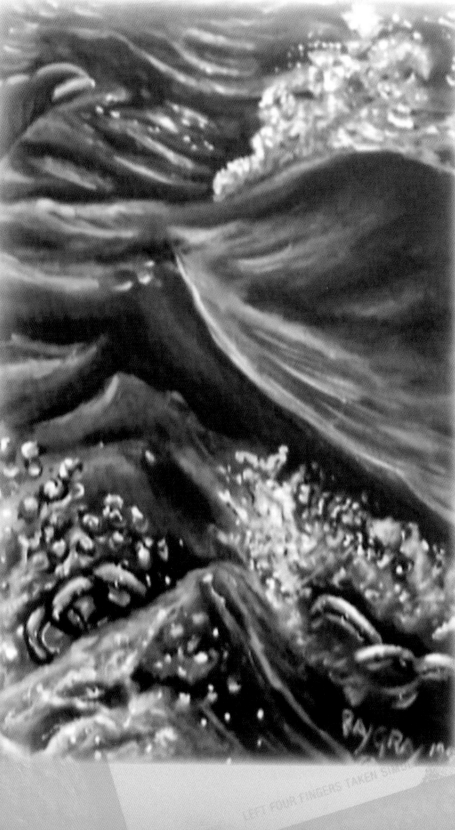

CHAPTER 5

WHEN REHABILITATION FAILS: WHAT HAPPENS AND WHAT CAN BE DONE?

Rikers Island is New York City Department of Corrections' largest prisoner facility. Considered a true penal colony, the island has ten separate jails that can hold a total of more than 16,000 inmates. In addition to its jails, Rikers has its own bakery, central laundry, tailor shop, print shop, maintenance and transportation divisions, marine unit, K-9 unit, and power plant. It's a land unto itself. And, sadly, it's a land to which its temporary citizens often return. Rikers has an incredibly high recidivism rate: according to one estimate, 80 percent of inmates who are released from Rikers Island are later imprisoned there again for additional offenses or parole violations.

Once an offender has served his sentence, society needs to do what it can to ensure he doesn't go back to his cell.

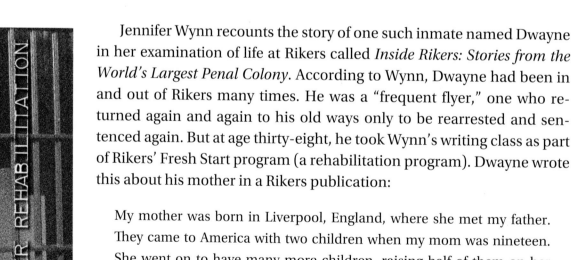

Jennifer Wynn recounts the story of one such inmate named Dwayne in her examination of life at Rikers called *Inside Rikers: Stories from the World's Largest Penal Colony.* According to Wynn, Dwayne had been in and out of Rikers many times. He was a "frequent flyer," one who returned again and again to his old ways only to be rearrested and sentenced again. But at age thirty-eight, he took Wynn's writing class as part of Rikers' Fresh Start program (a rehabilitation program). Dwayne wrote this about his mother in a Rikers publication:

My mother was born in Liverpool, England, where she met my father. They came to America with two children when my mom was nineteen. She went on to have many more children, raising half of them on her own. After several years on public assistance, she volunteered for Head Start, where she became a teacher's aide. She then returned to school and managed to graduate from college with a bachelor's degree—all the while being a mother to nine children and a grandmother to eleven. Today she's a teacher for the New York City Board of Education. She teaches children with special needs and continues to work toward her master's degree in special education. My mother is a very special lady, and I look to her for inspiration.

According to Wynn, since his last release from Rikers over two years ago, Dwayne has done something he's not been able to do before: he's kept a job and stayed clean. He's quit smoking and lost thirty pounds. He's done something four out of five Rikers former inmates can't do. He's stayed out of trouble. The author quotes his explanation: "The streets didn't get me again. . . . I didn't give them time to catch me."

This time Dwayne succeeded in staying out of Rikers. The difference, this time, was relationship: he enrolled in a live-in program on the day of his release from Rikers, was assigned a counselor, learned computer repair, and got a job—all of which involved ongoing stable relationships with people. He maintained his relationship with his writing mentor, another significant relationship. And, as he wrote in the article above, he recalled his mother, perhaps his most consistent relationship of all.

Unfortunately, Dwayne is the exception at Rikers. He's also the exception nationwide. The U.S. Department of Justice estimates that over two-thirds of America's inmates will return to prison or jail after their initial releases. Another study done by the BOJS found that, in a fifteen-state study, 67.5 percent of prisoners released were rearrested for a felony or serious misdemeanor within three years, while the vast majority of these were rearrested within twelve months of release. Of these, nearly half were convicted of their crimes and returned to jail or prison. According to the Corrections Research Solicitor General in Canada, where recidivism rates are better but still not good, the reconviction rate for inmates after release is over 40 percent. This phenomenon is what **criminologists** have termed "revolving-door justice."

When so many convicted criminals serve their time, get out, and then return to criminal behavior, it indicates that something in the American corrections system must not be working. Various North American corrections agencies (federal, state, local, and provincial/territorial) insist they exist not only to punish, but to protect, treat, and rehabilitate. And

Many offenders were once children who experienced poverty and dysfunctional homes.

WHO IS MOST LIKELY TO BE REARRESTED?

- former inmates who have been out of prison for less than a year
- offenders whose original offense involved property crimes (theft, for example)
- prisoners with longer histories of arrest
- those whose first arrest occurred before eighteen years of age
- younger prisoners
- men
- minorities

rehabilitation is supposed to equip prisoners for law-abiding, well-adjusted life beyond prison walls. When nearly one-half to two-thirds of those coming out of these facilities fail to successfully reenter their communities, their rehabilitation has clearly not been achieved. Why do so many fail to adjust to life outside their prison walls?

The detailed causes of high recidivism rates is a subject whose breadth far exceeds the scope of this book, but we can at least identify some general reasons why so many former offenders return to lives of crime. Consider the family backgrounds of offenders for example (sources: the BOJS report *Criminal Offender Statistics* and the Elizabeth Fry Societies in Canada):

- Nearly one-third (31 percent) grew up with a parent who was a substance abuser.
- Twelve percent had lived in foster homes or an institution.

- Almost one-half (46 percent) had a family member who had been incarcerated.
- One in ten men had been sexually abused.
- One in two (50 percent) women had been sexually abused.
- In Canada, over 80 percent of federally incarcerated women had either been physically or sexually abused.

Family of origin issues and family stability can play a role, as can experiences with others. Researchers have long asserted that an unstable home life, especially for juveniles, puts one at greater risk for becoming involved in or repeating criminal behavior. That's just part of the story.

Nationally recognized correctional training specialist Ned Rollo of OPEN, Inc., asserts that these seven factors most influence the post-release success (or failure) of former inmates:

1. criminal justice involvement (when, how long, and with whom you served; the nature of your incarceration experience)
2. awareness and self-understanding
3. self-control
4. values, attitudes, and self-image
5. survival skills and relationships
6. education and skills
7. determination and sense of duty.

While many other issues can influence the positive or negative development of these traits in an individual (mental health status, intelligence, social development, etc.), one basic issue, common to all human beings, affects them all.

Look through the list of seven factors again. As you read through this list, consider how many of these factors are impacted by relationship—or lack of relationship. Prison experience can be good or bad depending on the prisoner's relationships with guards and other inmates. Our view of ourselves can't be accurate unless others help us see those areas to which we are blind. Early family relationships impact our values, attitudes, and self-image—we get these from our parents, teachers, and

PRISONER REHABILITATION

Family stability plays a major role in future criminal behaviors.

caregivers. Education and skills come through training, and training is provided by other people. Some people motivate us to learn; others discourage us. Our instructors, bosses, and trainers (and the relationships we have with them) can prompt our growth or kill it. And a sense of duty comes when we realize our responsibility not only ourselves, but to others. There it is again: relationship.

As you read these brief stories quoted from *Hard Time: A Real Life Look at Juvenile Crime and Violence* by Janet Bode and Stan Mack (Delacorte Press, 1996), ask yourself this question: Did relationship play a role in the criminal behaviors described?

> I was going out with a guy named Jesse. Well, Jesse beat me. . . . I went through so much pain, but instead of leaving him . . . I'd do drugs until the pain would go away. One day my mom and dad were out of town. . . . Jesse wanted me to steal their bank card and my mother's four-wheel drive, so I did. . . . I got locked up in juvenile detention three months ago. I still love him and I always will. (Susie, age fifteen)

I was about eight [years old] my first time in court. Me and Shane, my brother, and some of his friends took the shingles off a roof and started throwing them at each other. Shane was four years older. He didn't really want nothing to do with me at that age. I was a pest. But he was my role model. Well, that day with the shingles, someone called the police. Three of us were charged. I was kind of excited this whole time. I felt, "Yeah, I'm up there with my brother." (Collin, age sixteen)

In her work, *When Prisoners Come Home: Parole and Prisoner Reentry*, University of California's (Irvine) professor of criminology Joan Petersilia cites Canadian researchers Gendreau, Little, and Goggin (1996) in determining the leading predictors of recidivism. The researchers mentioned several factors: some couldn't be changed (like history, race, family background, gender), but other factors (like substance abuse behaviors, interpersonal conflicts, personal distress levels) were able to be modified or adapted. Of the changeable factors listed (called "dynamic" in the study), "companions" was the leading factor in predicting whether or not an ex-offender would return to criminal behaviors. Who the ex-inmate surrounded himself with on his release made the biggest difference in whether or not he returned to a life of crime.

Who we hang with; the people who want to be with us; our "homies," friends, cohorts, buddies, partners, brothers, sisters—whatever we choose to call our closest circle of peers—these people influence us for better or worse. So do our families. When key relationships break down or are lacking, or when key relationships pressure us toward negative behaviors, we're more apt to do those things we thought we'd never do. It's no different for former inmates. When offenders leave prison without the support of good, law-abiding friends; when they leave the positive, encouraging environments of halfway houses or rehab centers to move back into bad neighborhoods infiltrated by drug dealers and gangs; when parolees or early release candidates have no one on the outside to remind them they're worth something or that they can stay straight, it's easy to see why so many ex-offenders reoffend. As one author put it, maybe corrections systems need to offer longer and more intensive follow-up services after inmate release, especially those that include men-

WHO IS MOST LIKELY TO BE SUCCESSFULLY REHABILITATED?

Offenders who . . .
- are willing to change.
- have a loving, supportive, law-abiding relational network on the outside.
- receive necessary substance abuse treatment and follow-up.
- acquire at least a basic education.
- learn a marketable trade or job skill.
- have jobs waiting for them on their release.
- maintain relational accountability after release.
- experience religious or spiritual motivation to change and stay clean.
- learn to manage their emotions in appropriate ways.
- have hope for the future.

toring or some kind of one-on-one personal, relational accountability and support.

Where the corrections systems have failed to offer this kind of relational support, private and faith-based organizations have stepped in. Many offer post-release follow-up services. Chuck Colson's Prison Fellowship, for example, offers Bible studies not just for inmates in prison, but for ex-offenders who are making lives for themselves after release. They also provide mentors and small groups where ex-inmates can have weekly accountability. Other private organizations, like the Elizabeth Fry Societies in Canada, help ex-inmates connect to people and places where

PRISONER REHABILITATION

In the Old West, offenders were thrown into jail for their wrongdoings. But even then, society wrestled with how to keep offenders from returning there again and again.

86

they can find inexpensive clothing (thrift stores), free medical and dental care, legal services, short-term and long-term housing, and support programs. Many programs and many organizations try to fill the gap, but no single approach seems to solve the recidivism issue once and for all.

As long as there have been prisons, society has wrestled with how best to help criminals change and return to their communities. Incarceration, as both punishment and rehabilitation, is only one method used not just in North America but throughout the world. Researchers, inmates, and those who work in the criminal justice system will agree, however, that incarceration, even with rehabilitation programs like those described in this book, yields mixed results. For some inmates, incarceration succeeds in transforming them; for others, it makes little difference in their likelihood of repeating crime.

In recent decades, alternatives to incarceration and rehabilitation programs have been developed and are being tried with mixed success, both in Canada and the United States. As is the case for most programs, some prisoners thrive in these alternative settings, while others return to lives of crime. One such program started as the unlikely result of a drunken vandalism spree in Elmira, Ontario (Canada), in 1974. Little did the teenagers who committed these crimes realize that their two-hour rampage would prompt the starting of a new organization called Community Justice Initiatives (CJI), and that this organization would be the first to start an alternative program for dealing with crime—an increasingly popular program called the restorative justice program.

PRISONER REHABILITATION

88

CHAPTER 6

REHABILITATION WITHOUT PRISON TIME? ALTERNATIVES TO INCARCERATION

When Russell Kelly was six years old, his father died. At fifteen, though he still hadn't come to terms with the loss of his father, Russ lost his mother, too. The parentless teen went to live with his older brother. Aching and "feeling unjustly victimized," as he put it in a *Stories of Reconciliation* profile published by Canada's Centre for Restorative Justice, Russ turned to drugs and alcohol to numb his pain.

Alcohol and criminal activity often go hand-in-hand, since alcohol diminishes people's inhibitions.

Alcohol brought out the worst in Russ. He'd get drunk and grow hostile, feeling a brewing rage deep within his soul—so much so, in fact, that he says he couldn't think clearly. His rage, he asserts, clouded his ability to think rationally or sensibly.

One night in May 1974, a then-eighteen-year-old Russ got together with friends to party and get drunk. The first part of their ruckus involved driving back roads for hours while they consumed nearly two cases of beer. Shortly after midnight the police pulled over the intoxicated teenagers, confiscated the remaining alcohol in their car, and told the boys to go home. After returning to the friend's apartment, the still-drunk teens decided to "raise some hell."

They sliced twenty-four tires.

They slashed car seats.

They destroyed one car's radiator.

They threw rocks through plate glass windows in people's homes.

They smashed the storefront window of a local beer store.

They hauled a boat into the street, punctured it, and flipped it over.

Crimes often escalate—from broken windows to more serious destruction of public property.

They pulled the cross from a local church display.

They damaged a gazebo.

They damaged a local traffic light.

They threw a garden table into a fish pond.

They destroyed a fence.

They smashed beer bottles through windshields.

Then they went back to the friend's apartment and passed out.

Their rampage lasted a mere two hours, from 3:00 to 5:00 A.M.

The cops were banging on the apartment door by 7:00 A.M., and Russ, who felt badly about what he'd done, immediately confessed. His case was handed to a probation officer named Mark Yanti.

As a religious man and a volunteer with the Mennonite Central Committee, Mark felt strongly about accountability and reconciliation. He felt that Russ and Russ's accomplice should meet the people they'd harmed. Mark asked the offending teens if they'd be willing to do this as part of their sentences. Knowing that if they didn't agree they'd probably face years of jail time, Russ and his partner in crime consented. The probation officer made a face-to-face meeting between the vandals and their victims a formal part of his recommendation to the judge who was handling Russ's sentencing. The boys' voluntary consent all but ensured that meeting the victims would be part of their probationary arrangement. The judge's order made it official.

In all, Russ and his friend damaged twenty-two properties. Instead of serving jail time, their sentence was to pay for the damages they caused, pay a *punitive* fine, serve eighteen months probation, and personally apologize to every person whose property they'd damaged or destroyed.

Mark describes what happened next in an article published by the Centre for Restorative Justice:

> Meeting the victims was one of the hardest things I had ever done in my entire life. Accompanied by our probation officer and a volunteer, we walked up to the victims' front door to apologize, hear what the victims had to say, determine the amount of restitution, ask for forgiveness, and assure the victims that they were not targeted. It was a random act of vandalism.

PRISONER REHABILITATION

A judge has the power to shape the future of youthful offenders' lives.

Some victims offered forgiveness while others wanted to give us a good whipping. Nonetheless, we survived meeting the victims of our crime spree and returned a couple of months later with certified cheques to restore the amount of out-of-pocket expenses not covered by insurance.

Today, Russell Kelly is a grown man bearing little resemblance to the angry teenager of that late-night vandalism spree. Though he never served prison time, he has not reoffended. In 2003, he graduated from the Law and Security Administration Program at Conestoga College in Ontario. He's happily married. And he volunteers with CJI, where he helps others work through conflict, mediation, and reconciliation.

Founded in 1974, the year of Russ's rampage, CJI is known worldwide as the first organization to start a restorative justice program. What Russ and his accomplice had to do by order of a judge when they faced their victims, sought their forgiveness, and made restitution, was the first time the idea of "restorative justice" was officially attempted in Canada. As

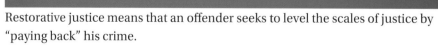
Restorative justice means that an offender seeks to level the scales of justice by "paying back" his crime.

a result of his experience with the two young offenders in 1974, probation officer Mark Yanzi went on to formalize the process the two vandals and their victims went through. That program is called the Victim Offender Reconciliation Program, and it's the hallmark program for CJI. Both practice the philosophy of restorative justice.

The term "restorative justice" sounds complicated, but it's not. It simply describes a means by which the person who commits a crime and the victim(s) of that crime are brought together in order for the offender to seek forgiveness and make restitution for his crime (pay back, if possible), as well as for the victims to address their attackers directly. It's a process that is increasingly replacing incarceration as a means by which to deal with criminals and their crimes. In Canada, it appears to be working.

Canada's solicitor general summarized one evaluation of the effectiveness of restorative justice programs to reduce repeat crime this way: "restorative justice programs can have an impact on offender recidivism that ranges from two to eight percent reduction for recidivism." His conclusion, based on forty-six studies of nearly 23,000 participants, reflects what those who practice restorative justice philosophies claim: bringing victim and victimizer together puts a personal face on crime that allows criminals to see exactly what they've done. Sometimes the relational component is enough to deter offenders from ever committing crime again. Just ask Russell Kelly.

Restorative justice programs aren't the only alternatives to incarceration that seem to be reducing repeat crime. A 1996 Canadian initiative called conditional sentencing is showing promise. A conditional sentence, somewhat like probation in the United States, is a sentence imposed by a judge on a convicted criminal wherein the convict must abide by certain rules, guidelines, and supervision, but serves his time in the community rather than behind bars.

Common conditions (or rules by which the convict must live) include reporting to a parole officer at regular times; remaining at home except for when the convict reports to his job or has medical emergencies; following a strict curfew; attending drug or alcohol abuse programs; paying

Community service might include something as simple as plowing driveways for the elderly.

INTENSIVE SUPERVISION PROGRAMS (ISPS)

ISPs are exactly what the name implies: programs where offenders are closely and intensively supervised. Though they serve their sentences outside of prison, the convicts, usually nonviolent offenders, are monitored closely. Most ISPs include:

- curfews
- mentoring or small-group peer support sessions
- specialized counseling sessions
- substance abuse treatment sessions
- some electronic monitoring
- telephone check-ins
- unannounced drop-by visits by ISP officers
- sometimes daily contact or check-in with supervisors

back his victims if the offender committed a property crime or theft; and performing a certain number of hours of volunteer work for the community. Generally, those serving alternative sentences are intensely supervised.

If the offender breaks any of the rules set down by the judge for him, he will be rearrested and brought back to court where the judge can send him to prison or impose additional conditions.

Conditional sentences are designed for less serious offenders. To impose a conditional sentence, the judge must be certain that the convict is not a danger to the community where she'll live. Most conditional sentences, therefore, are given to convicts who commit property crimes (theft, vandalism, etc.).

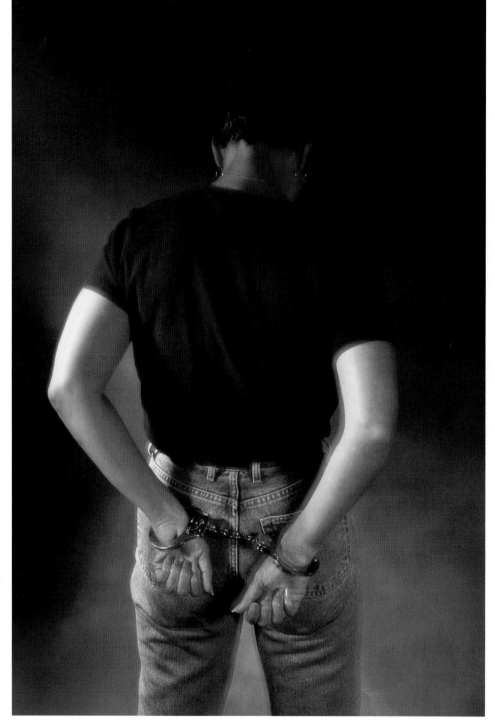

It costs more to send a teen to jail than it does to give her therapy.

Juvenile detention may not be the best alternative for a youthful offender.

Canada's Department of Justice found that in the three years between 1996 and 1999, Canadian courts imposed nearly 43,000 conditional sentences. Of those, only 15 percent (less than two out of ten) resulted in convicts violating the terms of their sentences and being rearrested. Even fewer (a statistically insignificant number) resulted in a convict's reoffense. The percentage of criminals serving conditional sentences who return to lives of crime is very small. Conditional sentences seem to work.

While these two imprisonment alternatives seem to effectively rehabilitate offenders who are involved in their programs, most criminologists agree that it is far better to prevent criminal behavior than to correct it after the fact. Prevention, they claim, not incarceration or rehabilitation or restorative justice, is the best way to build safe communities. In the United States, the Coalition for Juvenile Justice (CJJ) illustrates this position well.

According to CJJ statistical analysis, taxpayers save $2 million for each child who is prevented from beginning a life of crime. CJJ asserts that early education (preschool) programs increase a child's long-term

REHABILITATION WITHOUT PRISON TIME?

educational achievement and spares the public the $150,000 per year it would otherwise cost for that child's later criminal behavior. If the child does commit a crime, intensive probation during which the child receives consistent support and accountability reduces that child's likelihood of committing future crimes and costs one one-third of the amount of money putting that child behind bars would cost. Family-based therapy is another program CJJ promotes as not only a preventive to crime but as a tax-dollar saver. Most therapy programs cost one-tenth what it costs to send a teenager to jail.

Youth Villages, a nonprofit organization founded in Memphis, Tennessee, models CJJ's philosophies of prevention. Operating at thirty-three locations throughout Tennessee, Mississippi, Arkansas, Texas, and Alabama, its 1,100 counselors, teachers, and skilled staff help 5,000 troubled teens annually. By offering an array of programs and therapy methods, Youth Village staff workers can work with children with emotional and behavioral problems at home, avoiding the need for institutionalization and otherwise preventing criminal behaviors that might land these kids in jails or youth detention centers. In other cases, Youth Villages provides residential facilities for short-term crisis intervention or longer term care, both of which offer services to help the individual develop the skills she needs to become a healthy, functioning member of society.

Tammy, a one-time Youth Village resident, illustrates how programs like those at Youth Villages can prevent entrance into crime or the criminal justice system. Statistically, Tammy should have ended up behind bars:

Her parents divorced when she was five.

Her mother, with whom she lived, drank heavily.

As a young teen, Tammy started regularly using alcohol.

Fed up with her behavior, Tammy's mother sent her to live with her father.

Her father abused her.

Tammy ran away.

She was returned to her father.

He abused her again.

OTHER INNOVATIVE PROGRAMS

Instead of jail . . .

Fifteen-year-old Nathan served his time at a youth ranch raising horses in Idaho.
Eighteen-year-old Kara served her time at home with a monitor around her ankle.
Another offender planted and tended a garden in downtown Eugene, Oregon.
Clin restored a thirty-one-foot yacht in Florida.
A youth offender went to boot camp in Ontario.
And all completed their sentences and did not return to criminal behavior.

Tammy tried to commit suicide and ended up in the hospital for two months.

After experiencing such things, many young women like Tammy opt for life on the streets or resort to criminal behavior to get away from life at home. Many turn to drugs or theft or prostitution and end up arrested. Instead of doing what most teens in her situation do, Tammy wound up at a residential facility run by Youth Villages.

Today, Tammy is a primary school teacher, a mother, and a volunteer who works with teens. And she never ended up in the criminal justice system. The philosophy she learned through her experiences is one she now passes on to others, including her students and her own chil-

Youth Village offers young people like Tammy hope for a better future.

dren: "The biggest message I try to pass on to kids, including my own, is that it doesn't matter what your parents are like or where you come from. . . . Life is a matter of choices, and you are responsible for your choices. It's up to us to make our own lives better."

Instead of becoming another criminal justice statistic, Tammy became an illustration of how intervention and support can prevent a person from turning to a life of criminal behavior. As she put it, Youth Villages gave her her first positive experience of "family" life. Again, a loving relationship was key.

Youth Village offers young people like Tammy hope for a better future. In the best of all possible worlds there would be no crime, no prisons, and no need for rehabilitation. And everyone would have positive, loving support networks of family, friends, and loved ones. In the next-best world, one where crime exists, prevention would be the primary solution to problems of criminal behavior and the need for effective rehabilitation strategies. We don't live in a perfect world, though, or even the next-best thing.

In our world, where crime is a reality, prevention plays an important and effective role in the battle to redirect criminal behavior. Some people, however, still choose crime as a way of life (for an array of reasons). In these cases, it seems that a system including all strategies addressed in this book that work to any degree—incarceration, rehabilitation programs, education, behavioral incentives, job training, life skills training, feeling management courses, substance-abuse treatment, cognitive thinking therapies, and alternative sentencing options suited to individual prisoners—would be the most likely to effectively rehabilitate offenders. Just as no single cause can be identified as the source of today's criminal justice crisis, no single method or program will solve the issue. Perhaps if criminal justice authorities all over North America opened themselves to the possibility of making several strategies available, each tailored to suit an individual offender's needs, we'd be one step closer to more consistently successful rehabilitation.

GLOSSARY

agribusiness: Operations and businesses that are associated with farming.

catalyst: Somebody or something that makes a change happen.

criminologists: Experts who study crime, criminals, and the punishment of criminals.

euthanasia: The act of humanely ending the life of an animal.

hasp: A hinged metal fastener that fits over a staple and is secured by a pin, bolt, or padlock.

holding cells: Places where detainees are held pending court appearance.

incarceration rates: The number of people in prison per 100,000 population.

incorrigible: Impossible to correct or reform.

mentor: Someone who provides advice and support to a less experienced person.

metallurgy: The study of the structure and properties of metals, their extraction, and the procedures for refining, alloying, and making things with them.

mitigated: Made an offense less serious or more excusable.

parole: The early release of a prisoner, with conditions such as good behavior and regular reporting to authorities for a specified period.

proactive: Taking the initiative by acting rather than reacting to events.

punitive: Having to do with a punishment.

recidivism: The relapse into a previous undesirable type of behavior.

rehabilitation: Training or therapy given to someone to promote a healthy and productive life.

restitution: Compensation for a loss, damage, or injury.

sentence: A court's judgment specifying the punishment of someone convicted of a crime.

solitary confinement: Keeping a prisoner separate from others.

succinctly: Expressed briefly and with clarity.

supervised release: Release from a correctional facility under the watchful eye of an authority.

surrogate: Taking the place of somebody or something else.

values determination: Training to assist individuals in choosing what is most important to them in life in terms of moral choices.

FURTHER READING

Bode, Janet, and Stan Mack. *Hard Time: A Real Life Look at Juvenile Crime and Violence.* New York: Delacorte Press, 2000.

Chevigny, Bell Gale, ed. *Doing Time: 25 Years of Prison Writings.* New York: Arcade Publishing, 1999.

Gordon, Robert Ellis, and Inmates of the Washington Corrections System. *The Funhouse Mirror: Reflections on Prison.* Pullman: Washington State University Press, 2000.

Grapes, Bryan J. *Prisons.* San Diego, Calif.: Greenhaven Press, 2000.

Herman, Peter G., ed. *The American Prison System.* Bronx, N.Y.: The H.W. Wilson Company, 2001.

Lerner, Jimmy A. *You Got Nothing Coming: Notes from a Prison Fish.* New York: Broadway Books, 2002.

Prisons Almanac 2004. Washington, D.C.: Prisons Foundation, 2004.

Ross, Jeffrey Ian, and Stephen C. Richards. *Behind Bars: Surviving Prison.* Indianapolis: Alpha Books, 2002.

Stewart, Gail B. *Teens in Prison.* San Diego, Calif.: Lucent Books, 1997.

Williams, Stanley "Tookie." *Life in Prison.* San Francisco: SeaStar Books, 1998.

FOR MORE INFORMATION

American Civil Liberties Union (ACLU)
www.aclu.org

American Corrections Association
www.corrections.com

Canadian Centre for Justice Statistics
www.chass.utoronto.ca/datalib/codebooks/cstdli/cj2001.htm

Canadian Families and Corrections Network
www3.sympatico.ca/cfcn

Coalition for Juvenile Justice (CJJ)
www.juvjustice.org

Federal Bureau of Prisons (BOP)
www.bop.gov

Human Rights Watch
www.hrw.org

International Centre for Prison Studies
www.kcl.ac.uk/depsta/rel/icps/home.html

Justice for Girls
www.justiceforgirls.org

Juvenile Information Network
www.juvenilenet.org

National Criminal Justice Reference Service (NCJRS)
www.ncjrs.org

National Institute of Corrections (NIC)
nicic.org

PRISONER REHABILITATION

Office of Juvenile Justice and Delinquency Prevention (OJJDP)
ojjdp.ncjrs.org

The Other Side of the Wall
www.prisonwall.org

The Prison Policy Initiative
www.prisonsucks.com

Prisoners HIV/AIDS Support Action Network (PASAN)
www.pasan.org

Prison's Foundation
www.PrisonsFoundation.org

U.S. Department of Justice (USDOJ)
www.usdoj.gov

USDOJ's Bureau of Justice Assistance (BJA)
www.ojp.usdoj.gov/BJA

USDOJ's Bureau of Justice Statistics
www.ojp.usdoj.gov/bjs/welcome.html

Publisher's note:
The Web sites listed on this page were active at the time of publication.
The publisher is not responsible for Web sites that have changed their
addresses or discontinued operation since the date of publication. The
publisher will review and update the Web-site list upon each reprint.

BIBLIOGRAPHY

American Civil Liberties Union. http://www.aclu.org.

American Corrections Association. http://www.corrections.com.

Bode, Janet, and Stan Mack. *Hard Time: A Real Life Look at Juvenile Crime and Violence.* New York: Delacorte Press, 1996.

Canadian Centre for Justice Statistics. http://www.chass.utoronto.ca/datalib/codebooks/cstdli/cj2001.htm.

Canadian Families and Corrections Network. http://www3.sympatico.ca/cfcn.

Chevigny, Bell Gale, ed. *Doing Time: 25 Years of Prison Writings.* New York: Arcade Publishing, 1999.

Coalition for Juvenile Justice. http://www.juvjustice.org.

Conover, Ted. *Newjack: Guarding Sing Sing.* New York: Vintage, 2000.

Correctional Service Canada. http://www.csc-scc.gc.ca/text/home_e.shtml.

Coyle, Andrew. *A Human Rights Approach to Prison Management: Handbook for Prison Staff.* London: International Centre for Prison Studies, 2002.

Cozic, Charles P. *America's Prisons: Opposing Viewpoints.* San Diego, Calif.: Greenhaven, 1997.

Department of Justice Canada. http://www.canada.justice.gc.ca/en/index.html.

Federal Bureau of Prisons. http://www.bop.gov.

Gordon, Robert Ellis, and Inmates of the Washington Corrections System. *The Funhouse Mirror: Reflections on Prison.* Pullman: Washington State University Press, 2000.

Grapes, Bryan J. *Prisons.* San Diego, Calif.: Greenhaven Press, 2000.

Herival, Tara, and Paul Wright. *Prison Nation: The Warehousing of America's Poor.* New York: Routledge, 2003.

Herman, Peter G., ed. *The American Prison System.* Bronx, N.Y.: The H.W. Wilson Company, 2001.

Human Rights Watch. http://www.hrw.org.

International Centre for Prison Studies. http://www.kcl.ac.uk/depsta/rel/icps/home.html.

Justice for Girls. http://www.justiceforgirls.org.

Juvenile Information Network. http://www.juvenilenet.org.

Lerner, Jimmy A. *You Got Nothing Coming: Notes from a Prison Fish.* New York: Broadway Books, 2002.

Lionheart Foundation. http://www.lionheart.org.

Mauer, Marc, and Meda Chesney-Lind. *Invisible Punishment: The Collateral Consequences of Mass Imprisonment.* New York: The New Press, 2002.

National Criminal Justice Reference Service. http://www.ncjrs.org.

National Institute of Corrections. http://www.nicic.org.

Office of Juvenile Justice and Delinquency Prevention. http://www.ojjdp.ncjrs.org.

The Other Side of the Wall. http://www.prisonwall.org.

The Other Side of the Wall. *A Prisoner's Dictionary.* 2005. http://www.prisonwall.org/words.htm.

Petersilia, Joan. *When Prisoners Come Home: Parole and Prisoner Reentry.* New York: Oxford, 2003.

PRISONER REHABILITATION

The Prison Policy Initiative. http://www.prisonsucks.com.

Prisoners HIV/AIDS Support Action Network. http://www.pasan.org.

Prisons Almanac 2004. Washington, D.C.: Prisons Foundation, 2004.

Prison's Foundation. http://www.PrisonsFoundation.org.

Ross, Jeffrey Ian, and Stephen C. Richards. *Behind Bars: Surviving Prison.* Indianapolis: Alpha Books, 2002.

The Sentencing Project. http://www.sentencingproject.org.

Stewart, Gail B. *Teens in Prison.* San Diego, Calif.: Lucent Books, 1997.

U.S. Department of Justice. http://www.usdoj.gov.

USDOJ's Bureau of Justice Assistance. http://www.ojp.usdoj.gov/BJA.

USDOJ's Bureau of Justice Statistics. http://www.ojp.usdoj.gov/bjs/welcome.html.

USDOJ's Office of Justice Programs. http://www.ojp.usdoj.gov/reentry/welcome.html.

Williams, Stanley "Tookie." *Life in Prison.* San Francisco: SeaStar Books, 1998.

Wynn, Jennifer. *Inside Rikers: Stories from the World's Largest Penal Colony.* New York: St. Martin's Griffin, 2001.

INDEX

PICTURE CREDITS

Benjamin Stewart: pp. 12, 16, 40, 46
Corbis: pp. 72, 74, 98
iStock:
  Courtney Navey: p. 50
  Don Neudecker: p. 22
  Hon Fai Ng: p. 54
  James E. Hernandez: p. 36
  Jan Tyler: p. 86
  Jeff McDonald: p. 99
  Katherine Garreson: p. 52
  Matja Slanic: p. 102
  Nicholas Monu: p. 78
  Ronda Oliver: p. 96
  Sue McDonald: p. 37
  Tom DeBruyne: pp. 44, 49
Jupiter Images: pp. 14, 19, 58, 63, 66, 67, 68, 90, 91, 93, 94
Photodisc: pp. 15, 18, 27, 30, 31, 32, 34
PhotoSpin: pp. 80, 83

To the best knowledge of the publisher, all other images are in the public domain. If any image has been inadvertently uncredited, please notify Harding House Publishing Service, Vestal, New York 13850, so that rectification can be made for future printings.

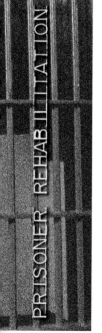

Chapter opening art was taken from a painting titled *Heritage* by Raymond Gray.

Raymond Gray has been incarcerated since 1973. Mr. Gray has learned from life, and hard times, and even from love. His artwork reflects all of these.

BIOGRAPHIES

AUTHOR

Joan Esherick is the chief writer for Lighthouse Educational Resource Network, a nonprofit foundation that provides education, life skills training, resources, and hope to those who face acute struggles in their lives. The author of eighteen books and numerous nonfiction articles, Joan resides in southeastern Pennsylvania with her husband of twenty-three years, their three young-adult children, and three Labrador retrievers.

SERIES CONSULTANT

Dr. Larry E. Sullivan is Associate Dean and Chief Librarian at the John Jay College of Criminal Justice and Professor of Criminal Justice in the doctoral program at the Graduate School and University Center of the City University of New York. He first became involved in the criminal justice system when he worked at the Maryland Penitentiary in Baltimore in the late 1970s. That experience prompted him to write the book *The Prison Reform Movement: Forlorn Hope* (1990; revised edition 2002). His most recent publication is the three-volume *Encyclopedia of Law Enforcement* (2005). He has served on a number of editorial boards, including the *Encyclopedia of Crime and Punishment,* and *Handbook of Transnational Crime and Justice.* At John Jay College, in addition to directing the largest and best criminal justice library in the world, he teaches graduate and doctoral level courses in criminology and corrections. John Jay is the only liberal arts college with a criminal justice focus in the United States. Internationally recognized as a leader in criminal justice education and research, John Jay is also a major training facility for local, state, and federal law enforcement personnel.

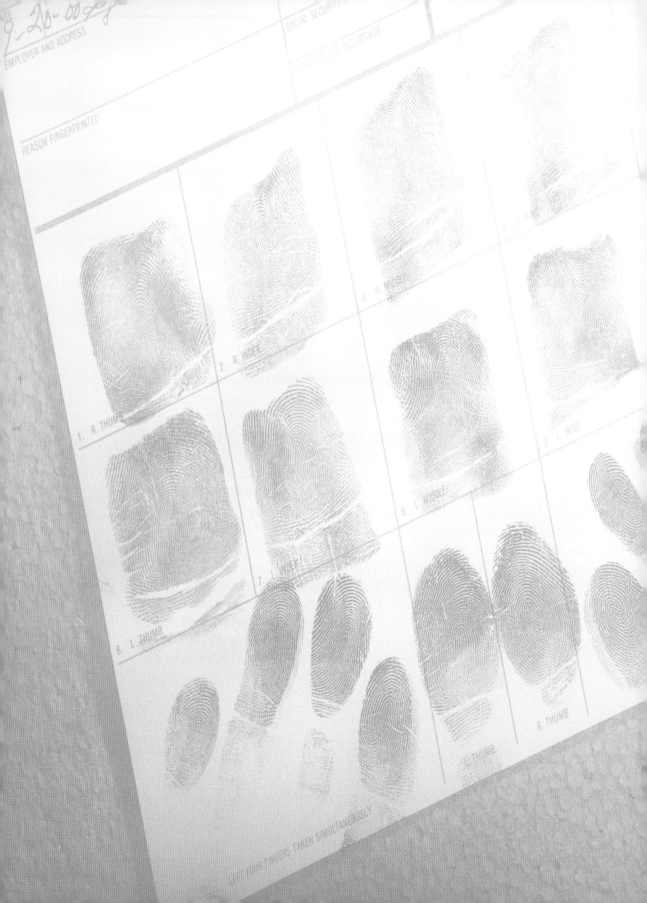